FOR UPS SHI

Edited by Douglas Glover

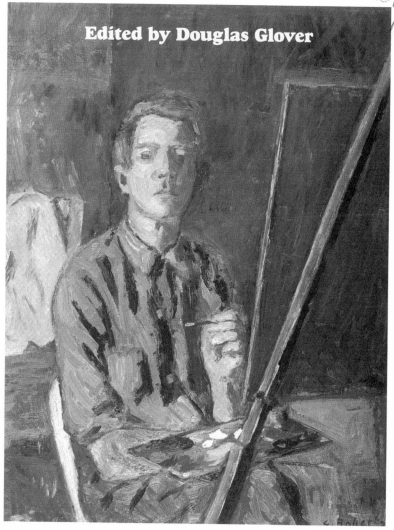

Best Canadian Stories
98

This book was written and published with the assistance of the Canada Council, the Ontario Arts Council and others. We acknowledge the support of the Canada Council for the Arts and the Government of Canada through the Book Publishing Industry Development Program for our publishing program.

Acknowledgements: "Three Diseases Requiring an Intermediate Host" by Kathryn Woodward first appeared in *Descant.* "Montana" by Dave Margoshes was originally published in *Prairie Fire,* as a co-winner of the magazine's long story contest. "Missing Notes" by David Helwig originally appeared in *Arts Atlantic.* "Buried Secrets" by Patrick Roscoe was first published in *Prairie Fire.* "Rumours of Ascent" by Gayla Reid first appeared in *Picador New Writing 4.*

The following magazines were consulted: *The Antigonish Review, Blood & Aphorisms, Canadian Author, Canadian Fiction Magazine, Canadian Forum, The Capilano Review, Descant, Event, The Fiddlehead, Geist, grain, Malahat Review, The New Quarterly, The New Yorker, Nimrod, Paragraph, Prairie Fire, Quarry, Saturday Night* and *Windsor Review.*

ISBN 0 7780 1099 6 (hardcover)
ISBN 0 7780 1100 3 (softcover)
ISSN 0703 9476

Cover art by Goodridge Roberts
Book design by Michael Macklem

Printed in Canada

PUBLISHED IN CANADA BY OBERON PRESS

There is a darkness out there (and inside)—source of all meaning. Usually, you can depend on consciousness to order the chaos of things, make it more palatable. The structure of language itself (the authoritative throw of the sentence, the demand for plot) gives the world an unwarranted air of symmetry and sense. Stories lie—always. Think of the words we use to describe the ends of stories: resolution, climax, denouement, recognition. Dreams. I've never had a resolution in my life that lasted more than five minutes.

The stories in this collection are often shocking, violent, gorgeously seedy, sometimes funny, and sad. When I look over the titles, the words "rumour," "secrets," "disease" and "missing" seem to insist upon a hidden significance. The best stories always resist the imperial violence of grammar, fight like hell against beauty and sense (in a language we might not recognize at first). And so we have Leon Rooke's pyrotechnic grotesque "There Are Bodies Out There" (about a bug, a hurricane and a teenage girl—among other things) which ends with a vision: "You could see them, Bud. Far out at sea. On the little rafts. All the burning virgins." And Ramona Dearing's "Itty Bitty Road" with its violent, hard-drinking, lips-like-whips heroine (a woman who insists, with every breath, every word, on being her bloody self, yes)—"Finally Pumpkin Puke turns around and I whale him one in the stomach. He squeezes my hands together and yells, 'What'd you do that for, love?' I'm screaming, 'You don't fuck with me. You don't fuck with me.'" And Mark Jarman's historical tour de force "Skin a Flea for Hide and Tallow" about a Métis refugee caught up in the phantasmagoric violence of Custer's Last Stand— "Horses with red hands and suns painted on their flanks stumble over bodies or shy away with crazy eyes as the 7th Cavalry's paper money blows around, hundreds of bloodied dollars decorating our bone orchard." And Dave Margoshes' "Montana"—the wondrously uneasy and surprising story of a runaway boy and a paedophile named Faust and a journey to a place of dreams called Montana but about as far from the real Montana as you can get. And "Buried Secrets," Patrick Roscoe's chilling tale of children, sexual fear, con-

7

tamination and muteness—"What there's no name for, no speaking of."

Are these literary terrorists or oracles? Or both? In some of the stories, the resistance to sentences is gentler, even humorous, though not less passionate. Yann Martel writes a delightfully sly piece—"Arithmetic and the Next King"— about an African chief, a missionary and mistranslation. "I was considered the Chibokwe language expert though I had been at the mission hardly five months." Gayla Reid's "Rumours of Ascent" is the dying meditation of a 70-year-old Australian woman who cavorts with death tigers in her hospital dreams while her lesbian lover insists on sending the newspapers reports of her miraculous ascension— "...the woman disappeared behind the clouds, then came out again, still going, on into the sky." In David Helwig's "Missing Notes," a middle-aged music teacher sees ghosts, receives enigmatic messages of violent death and promises unfulfilled, plays a piano with missing keys and hears the eerie tones of a lost music. "He was paralyzed, and the figure did not come to him, yet he thought that she was speaking and that he could almost hear a strange babble of words, or perhaps not words...."

What is the thing with no name? Where does the strange babble of not-words come from? Stories are a trap for something that lurks just at the edge of language, and the trap ends up standing for what it does not catch. At the end of her marvellous inversion of the traditional (male) African adventure story—"Three Diseases Requiring an Intermediate Host"—Kathryn Woodward writes: "On the stove a pot boils over, hissing and spitting. 'A message from the other side,' she whispers, and lets go the hand to attend to it."

DOUGLAS GLOVER

Contributions for the twenty-ninth volume, published or unpublished, should be sent to Oberon Press, 400–350 Sparks Street, Ottawa, Ontario K1R 7S8 before 31 January, 1999. All manuscripts should enclose a stamped self-addressed envelope.

Skin a Flea for Hide and Tallow
Mark Anthony Jarman

I never want to leave this country; all my relatives are lying here in the ground, and when I fall to pieces I am going to fall to pieces here—Shunkaha Napin (Wolf Necklace).

Schultz and the drunken Orangemen chased me out of Fort Garry with horsewhips and bayonets. I lit out for Pembina and St. Joseph, worked as a scarecrow gravedigger down around Fort Snelling and Sacred Heart Settlement.

Dig graves or starve. I could have eaten a folded tarp. I dug dirt for six years and now six seasons later I'm in a blue uniform riding into Montana Territory with that horse's ass Custer and a thousand arrows coming at me. Men I ate pork with last night twitch strangely on the ground and Brule children try to kill me in a thicket, laughing at me. More damn graves for someone to dig. Flint arrowheads and cuttin arrowheads break bones, open in you like a flower. Tin arrowheads are the worst.

After the bitter bad Sioux raids we moved warily on the troubled road between pillars of smoke to bury anyone we stumbled on. Could not tell sometimes if they were white or otherwise, bodies stripped and heads mangled or cut off or eyes scooped out with horn spoons. It takes a long time to bury a dozen or two dozen bodies, to dig holes for whole German or Norwegian families. Their pets or animals we threw into the high grass or into lakes with weights.

None of us on the side of angels. Both sides plunder and rape and both sides kill children (*nits make lice*). Both sides scalp, especially the escaped convicts and Missouri bush-

9

whackers and veterans of the war between the States; they are tough old dogs with knives hidden and nothing in life spooks them anymore.

The hangman was happy to hang dozens of Indians, charcoal and pigment still smeared on their faces; happy to hang almost anyone since Sioux had recently killed all of his children and his young wife.

I saw the merchant John Bozeman and his freighters and scouts killed by strange roving Blackfeet on his own road to Virginia City, the Powder River trail, the Bozeman trail, John Bozeman killed on the trail named after him, killed by his prosperity and industry in fur and gold. Sioux and Blackfeet didn't want him barging through the choicest parts of their beautiful country. They'd already seen it happen.

I could tell John Bozeman something about that, about losing my country.

The Orangemen with bayonets and horsewhips made me flee Fort Garry up in Canada, made me leave my family behind. The Ontario volunteers and the Schultz faction tried to kill me in the river with rocks. Goulet was murdered, murdered in our own land, as if we were the intruders.

They chased Fenians and Métis and hillsiders, chased anyone they didn't like the look of. Guilmette was murdered, they shot a priest, bayoneted Nault. They drank the country dry looking for wagon men to stab or shoot or beat or turn in for a reward, bothering poor Louis Riel's mother, turning her little house upside down every few days, in case her son was hiding there in a kitchen drawer.

A man back in Toronto was offering $5000 for Riel's head in a sack and any number of Christian razors wanted to collect.

I lived in Minnesota for about three years, then drifted west to Nebraska, along the shores of the Platte, and up to Deadwood with a shifty outfit of wolfers and reeking hide-and-bone men, teamsters and whisky-traders following more rumours of gold and all of us hungry men, all of us hungry. The government was about to open up the Indian

Territory, so let's get there first, right?

In talk by the tents and night firelight it comes out that I am a gravedigger by trade, and then the look in a fire-lit eye changes, every time, as if I am sizing them up for a coffin or a shroud, which I am not.

Now Indians in broken eyeglasses and with buffalo blood streaked on their cheeks are sizing me up, trying to provide me with a military funeral in the valley dust and sage and wild rose and crabapple. Is this my grave? Why then I'll fit ye, they seem to say. All this coming down on my skull because there were no jobs after the Panic of '73. I was skint, clawing wild bulbs and turnips out of the ground, scrounging coal left along the railroad. I was lousy, starving; but to think I asked to do this, to ride with Iron Butt Custer.

My cavalry horse was hungry and half dead when I finally shot the nag so I could burrow behind the hot belly and shoot savage nations and Jackie Lyons beside me doing the same behind his horse.

In the morning we rode down the ridge, down the slanting earth, and dismounted briefly, but Dreamers and dog soldiers roared at us like a threshing machine and we mounted again and climbed back up the ridge in a mad race, there to dismount once more. A cursed place to make a stand, no cover at all. What was Iron Butt thinking? Goes to West Point and all he knows how to do is charge and chase women, white or red. Damn your eyes, I swore, knowing my luck was running muddy, knowing we were bogged to our saddle skirts, Christ to be dead, and to know that, brain before the body.

One young soldier couldn't stop his spooked horse and it took him into the Indians, his horse's head out low and his head leaning back trying to turn the plug. How do you hide from five thousand Indians? Their tiny wild horses snapping like ugly dogs, savages lining up in the dust to get a chance at us, taking turns, more of them than there are fiddlers in hell. You'd need wings to get away.

I joined the U.S. Army with a false name because in 1875 they were taking anyone who could walk and chew gum. They didn't give a hoot. March green recruits around a sunny parade ground for a few days and issue rifles and let us hunt after Lo the Indian. Immigrants with no words of English, and ragtag ne'er do wells like me, seeking an army blanket and maggoty crackers and pocket money, though they never pay us when we're near a town with a bottle of tonsil varnish or a whore to lie with. I know how to ride and shoot from summers hunting bison with Gabriel Dumont but many recruits do not know a muzzle from a pizzle. I wish Gabriel and some others were riding with me.

Iron Butt Custer is supposed to be a sharpshooter but Bloody Knife joked that he couldn't hit the inside of a tent. I saw Custer shooting chukar in the Black Hills, though, and he looked a good shot. We were not supposed to be in the Black Hills. Looking for gold. This was asking for it. We found human skulls and a Canadian penny and cave drawings of strange animals and ships.

Custer cut off all his long hair for the summer heat and dirt and vermin; Custer took metal horse clippers to his head; maybe Iron Butt cut into his good luck when he cut his hair.

Hurrah, we've got them, the jackass Iron Butt said in the morning when he saw the circles of the huge village through the Austrian field glasses. Painted Nakota, Santee, Cheyenne, Blackfeet, Oglalas, Unkpapas in their peltry lodges, singing like dry axles.

Custer scribbles a message and gives it to the Italian, Martini.

"Is the man blind or poxy in the head? He'll have us all killed!" Jackie Lyons sputters. "Does he not see this coming on us and does he not care?" The papists and ex-papists among us crossing themselves, smelling brimstone and buckhorn-handled knives.

Three Crow scouts melted away after they noted the brevet General wanted to attack. No-one can call what we did an attack. Rifles jamming from dirty ammunition and arrows rattling down and I am thinking, Blast me, if these savages don't kill the ghostly blond fop I swear I will. Thinks he's so lucky that he can do anything, ride into hell's half acre with a few fop cousins and his pretty gilt hairbrush.

I'll crawl over F Company on my belly with a hatchet and kill Custer if the Indians haven't. Put a window in his skull. That would be a good trick: kill Custer and not be able to tell anyone I was the murderer.

Minutes or hours I have been lying on my stomach with five others in a circle, our heels touching. Marched half the fecking night for this, no sleep, bloodshot half-blind eyes, grumbling at each other on our dog-tired nags, nags hungry and trying to eat grass right until we shot them behind the soft ear.

Some lost their horses, and I still see the men trying to hold their horses' reins, boots wide, arms out and pulled, twisted, unable to stand and hold their reins in the mayhem.

I wanted to run when my companion Jackie Lyons took an arrow exactly in the spine—it sounded like it hit brick or wood and lodged there as he screamed out, as he reached around and touched the shaft and tried to yank it out of his backbone. Legs dead, face not his face at all, grey as his shirt.

Jackie's screaming does not aid my nerves.

A 16-shot Henry rifle and a Spencer carbine are firing to the north of us and I shoot over my poor screwbald horse until my rifle jams. I hit one savage with a shot right in the mouth and a goodly portion of his lower jaw flies away. He is wearing porcupine quills and a weasel tail. He has small-pox scars. This particular cut-throat does not fall but walks away from me without a chin, walks away as if he just re-called an appointment elsewhere. I don't know if I have killed any of the pirates. We seem to have little effect and they are merry as crickets.

Every few moments I look back at Jackie Lyons but I can't help him now, I have to watch the slope below us.

I tried to pull the arrow's shaft but the tendon tied at the top of the shaft gave way and the arrowhead remained driven into poor Jackie's back in sweat and blood. I get my knife out, not for his back but to clear my jammed rifle.

Something wrong with the ammunition or rifles. Spent shells won't pop out, making it hard to shoot more than once. These cursed Yankee rifles. I want to scream. We had better weapons with Riel in Fort Garry six years ago.

I'm sputtering and crawling around for another rifle when Connell and Howard make some agreement with their eyes, count out loud 1-2-3 (*why are they counting?*) as I'm crawling past and with Colt pistols shoot each other. God blind me, scares the hell out of me. Two shots and two heads half-destroyed. Couldn't the double-cunted arseholes shoot a few more dog soldiers before leaving the rest of us short of good men?

Arrows fly up in awful flocks. You do not know what arrows are like pulled back by strong men, by devils, and drawn in by us *wasichu*. A good bow can drill an arrow through rock or an army wagon. A storm lifts with its weird whizzing sound and drifts down in our legs and backs, pinning us to yellow prairie, snowflake horses and red speckled horses stepping through slim chokecherry shafts. Hundreds of arrows rattle and hum and I can't even see who is shooting them.

We were touching heels but finally no-one else is left alive but Jackie Lyons and his fecking arrow in his spine and me using someone else's Lancaster rifle behind someone else's horseflesh, in yellow land by a liver chestnut horse that could have been good, silver river looping below like an earring, wrinkled bluffs above my eyes.

We've got 'em boys, the blond ass said when first on the high ridge. We came here looking for trouble.

Jackie with his arrowhead is still screaming for Doctor Jesu and I tell him to be of good cheer and then I run away from yellow-eyed Jackie and the others, bolt like a coward from the bleeding bodies of my companions, run low toward a ravine that is already a graveyard for Smith's E Company.

My bootsteps seem so loud, everything noisy and slow, sliding into willow thickets and wild roses. My skin torn, lightning flashing up my elbow where it hits rock. Maybe I can hide in river thickets until dark, find the drunkard

Reno's men.

An Indian in a sailor's monkey jacket and a red woollen shirt dances, lifting a long sabre, but it can not be one of ours; we left our sabres packed in wooden boxes at Powder River. Indians in bear coats wave shiny government axes they were given as gifts at some peace parley. Thoughtful of the politicians to arm both sides in the fracas.

On the slope I see women using axes and knives and stone hammers on our fallen soldiers, see the women pull off the young soldiers' pants and slice at what is between their legs. Some men, pretending to be dead, jump up at that news, at that knife nudging their nethers. Some men jump up and the women and boys fall away from them, terrified of spirits back from the place. Some men jump up, then are hammered back down into the new world, the spirit world. No longer pretending. Shots ring out, hoarse voices call names. *John! John! Oh mother!* We fly and we crawl and we bleed. Horses flattened and gloves and hats and carbines around bloody pale bodies. It is June, summer in Montana Territory. I don't know how Major Reno is doing, where he is, how many of us are left.

I delve deeper into the draw's modest scrub willow, clamber on hands and knees in the red branches, shifting my hiding spot; young boys fire arrows into my thicket and the young devils laugh when I am hit in the calf and cannot help but yelp. Blood running in my hair and blood dripping from my leg and I am going to be killed by children with shining eyes. They find me amusing. They cannot see me but I lack dignity, an adult crawling back and forth like a clumsy blue lizard. Children with smallpox scars laugh at me and try to murder me as boys will with a frog or a snake in a bush, as I used to do with my cousins along the Red River, as the Orangemen did with poor Goulet.

I am panicking as I crawl about on hands and knees like a cur, not staying long in one spot, arrows and rocks crashing in the knobby branches. They toy with me, their laughter ringing my small refuge, and I am primed to give up hiding and run again when a green recruit from E Company, naked and bleeding from the eyes and crotch,

15

staggers past. He escaped the women with stone hammers but now my young boys chase after him with a whoop and a holler. Dripping with blood he looks so richly white, as if bleached by the diseased laundry girls that follow the 7th. We are rich in princes. A new victim is always more intriguing than the familiar victim. The poor bleeding recruit saves me for a few seconds.

I fall down in a flowered rocky draw, banging both knee-pans; crawl right into the rock, into a long crack that might protect me from the flint and gold arrowheads. Pushing willow back and I lie in the crevasse and let the ugly bush bounce back to cover my grave, and I shove flat pieces of sandstone and fistfuls of dust over my feet and legs and chest until only my French nose stands up to betray me. I am dead in the ground.

My knees and elbow and head throbs and the whole glinting river valley lit by low billows of dust and smoke. In the sky several suns drift; sundogs swim around them. I knew we should have stayed away from this country.

Riders with bloody masks and wolf voices and stolen blue uniforms sweep one way and others sweep back down until they hit a high riverbank or a coulee or a ridge and turn again, riders perched lightly on their mustangs as if playing on a piano stool. One horse drags the remains of some poor recruit. See what the ground does to you, the smallest bump or boulder. When that boy of ours falls to pieces the noble savages tie up another boy for their amusement and then that young boy falls to pieces on the bloody end of the hemp while his mother sits talking to a parson in a parlour in Ohio. This I watch from my grave of slatey stone and wildflowers, watch my friends torn apart, seeing too much, an underground man, knee high to a June bug, limp as a neck-wrung rooster.

Horses with red hands and suns painted on their flanks stumble over bodies or shy away with crazy eyes as the 7th Cavalry's paper money blows around, hundreds of bloodied dollars decorating our bone orchard. The Indians like silver, don't know paper money. Christ's foot I am thirsty and would give any amount of that bloody money for a cup of river-water or malt beer or even bluestone gin. We were paid day before the march, paid in the middle of nowhere so we couldn't run off. All this money useless to us here, useless to dead men. If I get out of here I'll hang onto a dollar, I'll squeeze it until that eagle grins. Or I'll spend it fast as I can, go on a jag of ribsteak and blue potatoes and growlers of Leinenkugel's ale every damn day and night till I die of a knife and fork, put down my knife and fork and big clay mug and lie on goosedown. Christ on a crutch I am thirsty. I slip grass into my mouth and pebbles in my mouth. Thirsty! Past sweat, my throat made of timber. I don't want a knife to my privates. I want a tumble down the sink. Why on earth do people want to cut up other people? I have seen too much of it on both sides. Why do the women like it so? I believe some of these Indian women would skin a flea for hide and tallow.

Our brevet General lived for a long time with a very young Indian woman, was sharing blanket duty with his brother Tom. I don't know if his wife Elizabeth knew; she may have. Lo the Indian, say the popular verses. Many of us, including Iron Butt himself, had to get the mercury treatment for the clap. Calamity Jane followed us wearing lice and the clothes of a man. Our deadbeat outfit was often drunk as lords, drunk as a boiled owl, trading coffin-varnish whisky to the Sioux for buffalo tongues and onions, or *grosse bosse*, the big hump those animals ferry for us like camels, or tender *dépouilles*, that tasty soft flesh under the ribs.

From inside my grave I watch as men I'd drank pine-top barleycorn with and ate bison tongue with and marched with wearing creased American boots have their private skulls broken into, like a head is a Chinese box, and their tongues and live brains pulled out and set up on rocks in some kind of display. Howdy James, Hello Will. The boys' arms are broken, feet cut right off, teeth chopped out with axes, and eyes turned into tiny tomatoes placed carefully on whited ledges. Our daubed and greased enemies don't want us to see or dance in the afterlife. I see Adam's apples cut from men's throats. They don't want us to have throats in the next world; no more crackers and tonsil varnish whisky,

17

songs and cursing. No Latin prayers or laughing drabble-tail whores. They want us to have nothing there in the afterlife, not a thing, not even a voice singing ballads about Garry Owen or a brain recalling the Panic of '73 that pushed me here in '76.

All those boyos who deserted over the months, got sick of army life and took the Grand Bounce, took French Leave, gone hunting for Montana Territory gold or hiring with the railroad or shooting buffalo for 40¢ a hide, Wellsir now I think them smart for clearing out, avoiding this, although many of those deserters may be long dead in other spectral greedy ambushes, boots yanked off their corpses and cut into pieces for the soft sweaty leather.

I think of my cousins up in Pembina and Batoche and St. Laurent and Duck Lake, running a flat-bottom ferry (*Best Scow on the River* says the poster on a poplar) and hunting and farming strips of land to the mahogany river's edge. A peaceful cabin with a lantern glowing yellow and blue in a parchment window. Batoche is not that far north of where I hide in this ravine. In a week or two I could walk there, call out from the yard. Remember me? The one who left? Show them my wounds.

I wait some time and the warriors seem to shift south to a copse of timber above the river, perhaps pulled to Reno's men or Benteen or to flummox themselves, and when they're gone a bit I rise from my grave and crawl north to where I started, where my dead horse lies, where I lost track of time, of early light and late light.

Jackie Lyons has dozens of arrows in him now. The arrow is gone from the hole in my calf though I don't remember pulling it. The Indians set up Jackie on his hands and knees and then shot arrows at his back end for sport. By running like a coward I missed that.

Pieces of bodies at my feet. Three heads cut off and arranged in a circle, staring sternly past each other, as if just finished arguing. Three heads and I know them. One bearded head used to play hornpipes on a cracked fiddle and you think, Johnny Reb, the ex-Confederate Irish Volunteer, why is your head bleeding red and black pitch on the dusty prairie? Laughing boys come to kill. Can I patch you boyos back together? You salty pilgrims squeezed through so many skirmishes and lung wounds and border wars, then Custer forced us in here. The bugle sounded for a while on this hill and then it stopped.

George Armstrong Custer is wounded but still alive just north of the three severed heads, Iron Butt Custer with blood coming out of his girlish mouth, Custer still alive with four dead officers sitting in a circle around him as if having China tea, and not with their men, their own companies. Why aren't they with their men? It is a strange scene, swallow-tailed silk guidons fallen on the ground, the blond devil alive and the dead circle of sycophants still trying to listen to him under clouds like ripped stunsails and golden light on the river and treed islands below.

When we first snuck in here I saw an Indian man peacefully washing a horse in the river; that seems so long ago.

Custer is shot in the side, just one wound that I can see. Custer's eyes are intense, one side in shadow, and he seems to be thinking hard, looking around but seeing God knows what. This vain man, famous for a handsome countenance, now looks like he'd been weaned on a pickle.

My skin is darker and coloured with blood and earth, my hair black, and I'm out of uniform, half-naked, a grimy wildman, but Custer calls as if we're old friends, as if we often shared lemonade and ginger-cakes in his tent with the cast iron stove that was so heavy to haul about.

"Trooper," he says to me, waving his pistol. "We've driven them off." Custer, at this moment, strikes me as someone who gets out of bed to turn over so his blankets last longer.

Custer cut his hair short before we left Dakota Territory and wrecked our luck, but his damn luck has held. He's had yet another horse shot out from underneath him but he's survived. Bodies bristling with arrows but not his body. Other have their entrails slip out and their entrails tied up with other men's entrails but Custer's white skin is almost pristine. Custer's famous luck.

I pick up his hat from the dust and skewed legs of the

dead officers. I'm going to keep the Brevet General's hat.

"Tom," Custer calls, "Tom, are you there? Boston? We must get back to Elizabeth. Autie, are you holding on? Where are my greyhounds?"

He is alive and mad in all this carnage. George Armstrong Iron Butt Custer looks very old. It's almost supper, I'd guess, and I'm very hungry and my eyes are sore. I need to take care of a small detail. He's still waving his pistol.

I move my hand slowly. With his own pistol and squeezing his own finger on the trigger I shoot George Custer in the temple and George Custer topples against one of the four men lying around him like a crib, smiling as he leaves a world. He looks happier. I expect more gore after what I have seen on this hellish hillside but the tiny hole in his balding blond head hardly shows. I assume there is more of a mess just inside that private place, inside his version of the Chinese box puzzle.

I help George Custer shoot George Custer and begin a long trip with a step, another step, limping north wrapped in lice, wrapped in a dead Indian's $20 blanket and wearing Custer's floppy hat, my bloody head where his bloody head was.

I dodge down into the next dip after our gory ridge, and what do I spy but a murder of crows and a spooked US 7th mare with the reins dragging and a picket stake bouncing behind on a hemp rope. Close by in the grass is a dead soldier with a hole in his face and his pistol lying by him and crows looking him over. I believe the crazy cuss got free of the aborigines, but shot himself, expecting a wave of them over the smoky ridge, believing himself doomed surely.

I pick up the suicide's pistol, catch his spooked horse and coax it toward Rupert's Land, toward Canada, coax my wrecked knee-pans, sky going crimson and yellow over the benchlands. I have some hardtack. I lost all my sugar and coffee and bacon back there, my letters and my crackers and molasses. I used to have anything I wanted when I was younger, anything, and it meant nothing at the time.

Nights I hobble the horse, trying to sleep before the hard-mouthed mare gets too far away, riding and walking on my sore legs, my bashed knees, the two of us fording or swimming the Yellowstone and the Redwater and the Missouri and Poplar Creek, drinking from a river and waiting for the next stream or lake to drink, crossing squatting hills of creeping purple lizards and red rattlesnakes and roses and berries that haven't ripened yet, watching redtail hawks and buffalo wolves and the poisoned carcasses, walking the suicide's tired horse toward Montagne de Cypres and Batoche and peace with my uncle and Dusfresne and Father André. Keeping grassfire smoke to the south of me, pushing north, sun burning me badly despite Custer's hat.

Beside a small creek I drink and then attempt sign language with three Indians in the skins of beasts who talk of the crazy whites shooting each other or cowards who threw their weapons away weeping, and I thought of my rifle jamming and I want to weep and curse again. They all know within hours what has happened, pluck the news from the air. Their scalp-locks stick up. Like a dream they surprised me at the stream. Are they Crow? Cree? I hope so. The stream likely has no name. The three men examine me and my horse with suspicion, mumble about my suicide's pistol and my knife, an old Arkansas toothpick. My blanket is full of lice. My skin is burnt black, blisters and pustules rising on my nose, my lips swollen. I listen to them and keep my burnt mouth closed.

Sioux did not kill Custer, I want to say. Lakota, no. Cheyenne did not kill Custer. Rain in the Face did not kill Custer. White Bull or Wooden Leg did not kill Custer. Hump did not kill Custer, Crazy Horse or Spotted Eagle did not kill Custer. Tantanka Yatanka and the Dreamers did not kill Custer. I killed Iron Butt. I want to steal it from them, own it like a seized pocket-watch.

I have Irish blood, Scottish blood, Cree blood and French blood. I wish to keep that mixed blood safe inside me, keep it apart from the dust of this destroyed summer where grasshoppers replace buffalo.

I still have my hands and feet. No-one has chopped them off. No-one has hammered my teeth out with a rock or set up my brain or eyes on a rock table.

Iskotawapoo, they wonder: fire liquid, blind tiger. No, I insist, No, for these three will kill me if they think I'm a whisky trader and I'm alone. I could use a drink of blind tiger. I don't want my face to betray that the suicide's pistol has no bullets left. If it enters my mind it may enter their mind.

If I can get back over the border, I'll settle down near Batoche, a gentleman farmer playing a cracked fiddle like Johnny Reb. Wolfskins stretched and lantern glowing yellow and blue in a tiny window and no more stone hammers to the brains, no more Orangeman horsewhips or bayonets at my backside. No more hacking and reeking trouble. I am from north of Assiniboine and I can keep my mouth shut, not like some of these Texans in the 7th.

The lice in my blanket trouble me. I see an anthill. I stir the anthill with a willow branch, churning deep, irritating them, and then I lay my blanket down on the dirt as the three watch my naked back. Frenzied red ants, streaming out to defend their ruined home, pick the lice clean from my borrowed blanket.

They'll leave us be in Batoche. Isidore and Jean and all my uncles and aunts and cousins dancing in my poplar cabin so snug you can't curse the dog without getting fur in your teeth.

Railroads gone broke and ants picking off lice and these three with greased scalp-locks looking at my naked back and wondering whether to kill me or let me cross.

Itty Bitty Road
Ramona Dearing

I'm about to get us a drink, I'm just leaning in to order it when this guy next to me says, "Careful there, love." And I'm thinking if he says one more word to me, if he says boo, if he even sneezes, I'm going to tell him to fuck off. Because a) no little shit sniggers at me and b) I especially don't like this little shit's rat-pus teeth.

Beer is a buck, you can have any kind you like as long as it's Blue and as long as it's in a can. Drinks are a dollar a double, which is why me and Mitch always get rum and Pepsi. Like Mitch says, get a beer, you're throwing 50¢ out the window.

Arsehole's eyes are still velcroed on me while I wait, he's poking his buddies and his face is cracked with laughter, like he's proud of his tea-stained piss-stinking teeth or something. The bartender pushes my drinks over and when I reach for them he crooks his finger like he's got something important to tell me so I lean in and he screams in my ear, "Haven't you read the sign?" And the boys are going ooga ooga like they're going to crap their pants.

I look up but I don't see it and then I look over and there it is. *No Boobs on the Bar.*

So yeah, welcome to the Bulldog. Home away from marvellous home for the Royal Air Force.

They have two clocks behind the bar, one on Labrador time, one on Greenwich Mean. They drink a toast to the Queen at midnight their time, and one to Diana at midnight local time. Mitch and I have only been here for the Di one. They turn down the music and three or four guys try to grab the microphone and whoever wins walks around with it mashed against his lips. The guy'll say stuff like, "You fine, fine lady, you're wanting a real man, I think you're wanting a real man such as myself. Chuck's not a man, you need a good man, I think I could do you some good." Sometimes it strings along for five minutes. The last line is always the same: the guy with the mike says, "I love you, Di," and everyone in the bar lifts their drink and says, "I love you, Di."

Mitch always says, "I loathe you, guys," just before he drives his glass into mine.

But we like it here, me and Mitch. They play the Clash and they play Adam Ant. Which, as Mitch says, is something around here. Plus it's the only military club you can get signed into without dropping someone else's name. Anyway they just sit around and say *yah, yah* at the German club and drink this dark beer like they're fondling it. The fucking kooks are in love with this brown beer. At the Canadian club, the guys wear Mickey Mouse ties. At the Mac club, the Americans wear slitty little black leather ties, and Mitch has never explained why exactly, but he gets homicidal in there. Which is fine, because I'm not into silk shirts and pleated pants. Also, I'm engaged to Sammy and I'm not supposed to be into anything.

Mitch keeps saying, "He'll never know," like it's a big joke. Just because all the other guys around here are sharks doesn't mean Mitch is any different.

So we do the Dog. Ten bucks each, we're smashed and we still have cab money. You can't go wrong. There is that tooth thing, I figure something like half the Brits sucked tar instead of tits when they were born. And those same guys are all short. They're also jokers. They don't believe you when you show them the engagement ring and tell them a big man is going to dip his toe into their belly buttons and feel around for their spines.

"That's just a line," they say. "That's just a ring. All girls have rings."

It's my grandma's engagement ring, she always wore it even though my grand-dad left her and moved in with another chicky. Not much of a ring, really. Grand-dad never really did wet his pants for Grandma. She made me take it to keep the military boys away. I've had perfume that worked better. Sammy says there's a real ring coming. That's what he said, I'm only repeating it.

"So boobs on the bar means you have to buy a round," Mitch says. Then he says, "I guess with your build it's hard not to."

I'm shaped like a coffee can. Not like Mitch is the Man from Glad or anything. His shirt is always untucked over his belly. Which feels okay when I slap my hand on it, my cold rum hand.

—Hey.

—Who's carrying too much what?

—Come on, it was a compliment. You're nicely laden.

—What?

—You're well-laden.

—What?

—Laden. L-A-D-E-N.

—Oh. Yeah, and wouldn't you like to set my table.

—Indeed I would.

He talks like that, if he's talking about a court case he's covering, he'll say something like, "The man thought his only choice was to steal the money. Sadly, he was wrong." Or he'll say, "It's a sombre sky, don't you think."

Sammy's not like that. He talks the same as everyone else. Never shuts up, actually.

We're standing by the emergency exit, Mitch is smoking out the door. It's not too cold, springtime in Siberia. Lights are moving up and down the runway. Like a bunch of coal miners practicing for a funeral or something.

"Innu," Mitch says. Every year they block the runway. The military police are doing a sweep. "Good," he says, "needed one more item for the paper."

"Come on," I say.

They're playing "Anarchy in the U.K." I push Mitch ahead of me and when we get to the dance floor he sticks his cigarette in his mouth and leans back like he's trying to get the smoke away from his eyes. I'm the only girl out there, the Brits are dancing boy-boy, they're slamming each other and running up behind each other's backs and giving themselves boosts. I see one guy's shoe wedge right between another guy's shoulder-blades. Then they put on "God Save the Queen." And more guys come up. The tall ones with good hair, the beauty boys.

And then an elbow or a knee or something tries to iron out my cheekbone.

Mitch is saying, "Come on, Lucy," but I'm tapping this redhead on the arm and poking harder each time. Finally Pumpkin Puke turns around and I whale him one in the stomach. He squeezes my hands together and yells, "What'd you do that for, love?"

I'm screaming, "You don't fuck with me. You don't fuck with me."

In the cab, Mitch says, "You know, you've really got an aggression problem there."

"No fucking kidding," I say.

We're coming up to the base gate.

"That's something around here," I say.

He starts laughing. He leans over and rubs my hair like I'm a goddam dog.

"Quit that shit," I say and he puts on a big pout, but from tonight on he calls me Scrapper.

So I don't know if you've figured it out yet, but Mitch is hurting for me. He wants me so bad I bet his lips are bruised from saying my name. It's no trouble to see the way he looks at me like he's trying to put the brakes on, but what's the point because the truck's going over the edge. And what do you think of his finger poking the left cheek of my ass like he was trying to make a dimple (while he was supposedly bending over to tie his shoe)?

—Uh. Sorry. Sorry.

That's what he said. The man's afflicted. And if it weren't for Sammy (and okay, maybe Sammy's navigator, pretty good with directions I always say), I'd be getting dimples carved into my ass with the pointy end of a potato peeler, and I'd be showing Mitch my longjohns. What with Sammy working in Yellowknife and all, I've had a hard time keeping my trapdoor shut.

I kissed Mitch one night. I thought he was awake, just lying back listening to Bob Dylan. Mitch is always saying I should stop talking for a while and just let the lyrics go through me, so this one night I sit there nice and quiet but I don't listen. To what? Like hey, I'm Bob, hey listen, hey hey hey hey, I'm Bob. I'm so wise and I'm so big and I'm so fucking nothing.

What I'm doing is leaning in, sneaking over to Mitch's side of the couch and I'm looking at his face for a long time. I swear I can feel his cheek before my lips touch it. He doesn't open his eyes, so I go back to my corner.

But later on he says, "When's Sammy coming back?"

So tell me that's a coincidence.

June is a weird month. Once I went into a dance at 10.30 and there was still light in the sky and when I came out at two there was blue at the other end of the sky. If you don't go home until after four, you're fucked. You can't sleep, unless you do hot-knives.

I'm calling and calling Sammy, he's never home. Guess he's not sleeping much either. Better not be some bitch involved. She wouldn't look good with a face full of scabs. He wouldn't do that to me, I don't think. Although his dad was hard at it all the time, everyone knew that. Sammy, he'd rather go out to the cabin for a weekend than be ripping teddies off of me.

I miss him snoring in my ear. I miss how he tries to make me late for work by making me breakfast in bed and not letting me get into the shower until I've eaten every last hashbrown. I miss how he gets mad at me when I let off and plow someone, even if it is a total asshole.

"I can't take much more," I tell Mitch. "A girl has stuff inside that'll bust if it doesn't get used."

"Oh my, couldn't have that, could we? A strapping milkmaid like you."

Mitch is the only guy who's allowed to laugh at me, even

27

if I don't get it.

He says, "I've been thinking about how I miss parkas. I want winter to come back fast. I do this thing when I'm waiting in a line-up at the Northern store or wherever, I pretend the women are all naked under their parkas, and I give them one long zip. One long, extremely mysterious zip."

—Yeah, so. I want to have sex on a skidoo.

—Better still, on an ice-pan. A couple of sleeping-bags, that'd be peachy.

—Ever done it on a bus? That's pretty good too.

—Um, no.

We're driving onto the base, going to a movie. The Arcturus theatre has this ugly white parrot in the lobby. Its cage has shredded paper inside, straight from the Colonel's office, Mitch figures. Once some pieces were sticking out the sides and Mitch shoved them in his pockets. He always says, Tell me what you know. Tell me what you know, Pretty Polly.

Its name is really Flummy. They say the only words the bird can say are *caribou* and *stew*. Flummy is kind of fucked-up and squawks during kisses and shoot-outs. Seeing as the movie is *Terminator 2*, the bird is having a bad night. So is Mitch. He isn't saying much when we get in his truck.

"We should have left," he says. "What possessed us to stay for that?"

I say, "It was kind of bad, but no point putting your balls in a noose or anything."

Mitch looks like he wants to hit something.

"What's this?"

The base has all these back roads, places where people go berry-picking or take their dogs. We're at the intersection of one of them and Mitch wants to turn left but a big chain is swinging across the road, with a no-trespassing sign next to it.

Mitch turns around, drives some more, we hit another chain. He sits there with his foot on the brake, his head on the steering-wheel.

—I just want to drive somewhere, Scrapper. All I ask is

28

to go for a little drive.

And he looks so lonely I want to squish him between my boobs.

—We could go to 'Striver.

Which is as far as you can go by road and I'm hoping he'll say no because I don't think driving for half an hour and then turning back is going to make him feel like a lottery winner. I can see the shit Bruce Springsteen would write if he lived here. "Same Old Road." "Itty Bitty Road." "Same Old Itty Bitty Road."

"Nah," Mitch says, "I've got an idea."

A plane is going over. Commercial, not a fighter. They fly in daylight in pairs. There's enough of a glow in the sky the body shines like a lightbulb in a fridge.

"Think it's going to Halifax?" he says.

—Fuck no. Chicago.

—Beijing.

—Panama City.

—Lisbon.

It's this little game we play all the time.

He starts the truck, smiles and waves at the guard at the main gate and says "fuck you" between his teeth. In the Valley, we pick up some beers and drive onto the beach.

What I want to know is why does everyone in the entire world start twirling around and running in these big lunky circles when they're on beaches, even when they're pathetic beaches? When we get tired, we squat down and drink some beer. We drink one at a time, passing it back and forth. I'm thinking Sammy baby, why didn't you phone me, why didn't you phone because I'm maybe, possibly, yes, going to be a very bad girl tonight.

—Scrapper?

—Yeah?

—I'm cold.

—I gotta piss.

—So piss.

—Where?

—Surely you're not one of those girls, Scrapper.

—Suck my butt hair.

29

I walk till I can't see him anymore, only the red of his cigarette, before I drop my pants.

"Come here," he says when I get back and he's pounding the sand beside him. He puts his arm around me.

"Guess that's a story, those gates," he says. "They're afraid of the Innu. It's going to be quite the summer. Quite a good summer."

I tell him about Sammy that time. He's driving down to 'Striver, it's early winter, only about minus ten and there's this guy hitchhiking at the halfway point. He doesn't have a coat on so Sammy pulls over and tells him he'll take him to Shetshatshit. And everything's fine for a couple of minutes but then the guy starts talking and he's high on something. Not booze, Sammy says, he was talking too clear and fast, he just wasn't making sense. So Sammy says uh huh a lot just to be polite. All of a sudden the guy has both hands wrapped around Sammy's neck and he's not killing him but he's not hugging him either. Sammy doesn't know what to do. He's got a bag of chips and Sammy says, hey buddy, would you like some? And the guy lets go of Sammy and starts porking and Sammy takes him home.

No fucking way I'd be all nice-like to that loser but Sammy gets all holy about Doing the Right Thing. Sometimes I figure I'm one of his projects too. I trust him best when he's drunk, then I know who he really is. Not very nice, and not too skanking worried about it. Which is me, that's my life every day. Except I have a couple of rules. I don't hit anyone wearing glasses and I don't even so much as yell at someone I respect. Because otherwise, where are you? Sammy gets his rules all mixed up when he's on the beer.

"Fucking Indians," I say, "they should put them somewhere and keep them there."

—Jesus, that's enlightened.

—They're ugly and lazy and fucking users. Use everything they can until there's nothing left.

—How do you know that? How can you say that? Do you know what it's like for them?

—And they're fat and smelly and I'm tired of seeing

them on TV.

—Stop.

—It's my land too, it's my place. I'm not going to fucking stand by and let them eat fried chicken all the time and leave their stinking diapers everywhere. Not on my land, Mister.

—Shut up, Lucy.

—What's the matter, gone native? Got a hard-on for some squaws, do you?

—Stop it.

—You'll have ugly, fat, greasy babies.

—Stop it. Just stop. I'm not listening to this shit.

—And they....

—Will you fucking stop it now. STOP. Close your fucking filthy mouth.

He doesn't have to go crazy like that. It's just a conversation.

We sit not looking at each other, not drinking beer. No arm cozy around me. My butt is grinding into the sand.

Finally he says, "How's the job going, anyway? You never talk about it."

—It's just one big joy-ride after another.

He smiles a little.

—Scrapper.

We sit a while longer. He puts his arm back around me, tight around my shoulders.

He says, "Keep a secret?"

—Yeah, sure.

—I'm getting married as soon as I get transferred out. I'm like really, really nervous.

—That's wild. Congrats and all that shit.

The next time we go to the Bulldog, I kick this idiot in the shins when he sticks his hand on my ass. I tell him he's lucky I'm in a good mood or he'd be written up in all the medical journals as the guy with a dick that goes in instead of out. Then I drag some schmuck home with me, it's not even midnight, they haven't done the toast to Di yet. I'm holding him by the sleeve and I take him over to where

Mitch is standing.

—I'm splitting.

—Okay.

And then he leans in all concerned-looking and says in my ear, "But what about Sammy?"

I say, "Never mind the bollocks," and we're out the door. Sammy who? Hasn't phoned. Doesn't care.

I smell bitch.

Mitch and I don't talk about these things. Except once he shows me a picture of his chicky-poo, she lives in Halifax. Put it this way, if I were a guy, I'd fuck her. Mitch says she plays flute and that he wishes she'd fatten up a bit.

His fucking cat. A leg-hold trap would be too good if you could find one anymore. Mitch thinks this cat is Marilyn Monroe in a litter box, calls the thing Bauble. The fucking thing bites me whenever Mitch isn't looking, follows me into the bathroom, backs me up against the wall and chomps away at my ankle. And all I can do is stand there and tell myself to breathe. One time I had to beat it off with the toilet plunger.

You're probably thinking, what's a big-boned girl like you doing afraid of a stinking cat. First of all, you've never met Bauble. Second, I bet you have your own thing, like moths or cliffs or ladybugs.

Okay, if you're afraid of ladybugs, you're an asshole. But everything else counts.

"Mitch?" I say. I'm sitting in this old rocker with two spindles crunching into my spine and I'm watching him rub the cat, which is vacuum-sealed to his chest and Mitch is KISSING the cat and I'm watching these long white hairs float around the room and the rocking-chair doesn't even move right because of the carpet.

—How come we never go to my place?

—Because you're a slob. And your music sucks.

He goes back at Bauble. I keep trying to make the rocking-chair go. A lot of times we don't talk much but I know he wants me there. After a while, flea-whore jumps down.

Mitch says, "If we lived in, say, Philadelphia, and somehow we'd been introduced to each other, do you think we'd associate?"

—Associate?

—Yeah, hang out. Do this.

—Yeah.

—We would?

—Yeah.

—Really? Really truly? Why?

—Because I know we would. We're meant to be stuck in some shithole somewhere together.

—I don't know. In fact, I can say with some assurance that anywhere else except here, I would not talk to you. I'd be scared of you, Scrapper. I probably wouldn't even like you.

—Yeah, I'd be too much for you. I'd be too fucking real for you.

—But you are, how shall we say, a diamond in the rough. That's kind of what you are, at least to me.

I don't say anything. Sometimes the smartest way to get someone to yap the goods is to shut up and stare.

—Which is to say although I hate this place, at least you're here. Despite your tendency to commit assault and battery on a regular basis.

I see the pillow coming just before it hits my head. Nobody throws shit at me and lives. I pin him on the couch.

—I'm going to give you a wedgie for that, you bastard.

He laughs so much I lose my strength. And he pushes me off when I don't expect it so I land on the floor doing a form of the splits. He looks down at me from the couch, still laughing.

He says, "I'd never ever talk to you. Even if you asked me what time it was, I'd just keep walking."

Three Diseases Requiring an Intermediate Host

Kathryn Woodward

Eighty days, Philip once breathed into Iva's ear. In 80 days a single person can produce 5000 new infections.

The statistic explained why Philip left her for days on end to tramp through the bush spraying DDT. To Philip, heroes were men who held out their arms and allowed themselves to be bitten for a cause. In this case, malaria. Its peculiar, leisurely transmission. The meandering pathway from man to mosquito to man. Once we knew this, Philip whispered fervidly, the end was in sight.

Just around the corner, they both believed.

In 1965, the World Health Organization transported Philip from Vancouver to their station in Liberia. Philip was 28, Iva 21. There was no question of Iva finishing her final year at university and joining Philip later. Nothing she studied could compete with such opportunity To Do Good Work. She could get back to the elements on the periodic table another time, when she finished globetrotting. *If* she finished globetrotting. Iva hurriedly filled a trunk and two suitcases. She and Philip boarded a plane directly from their wedding. They flew first to Geneva for Philip to be briefed. A Brit met them at the airport there. Last lap of luxury, he called their hotel, making them feel important.

They squeezed themselves into a metal cage and rode to a room where flora ran amuck—covering curtains, bedspread, walls.

"An outbreak," Iva said, dropping her bags.

"A pandemic," Philip chimed in.

They were tired but elated and expectant. Mercifully, the sheets were white. Iva drew the blankets back. She and Philip undressed and lay down.

Philip began at her nose, her proboscis in his vocabulary. He ran a finger from it along her mouth, down her neck, between her breasts. His penis hardened as he stroked the silky skin of her abdomen, site, Iva now knew, of the first wondrous malarial incubation. He then retraced his steps, bending over Iva this time and using his lips. He stopped briefly under her chin, at her salivary glands, because that was where the anopheles mosquito stored the ripening malaria. Now Philip became this mosquito and Iva the victim. He bit her gently, murmuring how important it would be for them to sleep under netting once they reached Liberia. He trailed his mouth to her liver, site of the second incubation, and then, lifting his head, mounted her.

In subsequent days it was at this point that Iva thought she heard a faint cheer rising from the floor. From the paperwork strewn over the blooms on the carpeting, statements from sufferers made to talk, those who already had had their spleen rates correlated and their parasites graphed. Philip's Liberian sufferers, the ones he had been assigned to, were not as yet catalogued. That would be Philip's achievement, punching holes in Parasitological Surveillance Cards: tribe and sex; fever: yes or no.

Iva knew that a body as portentous as a world health organization would meticulously vet any potential employee before declaring him fit to hire. But still she worried. Philip was so slight a man, and he had such milky eyes and pallid skin. The darker, hardier-looking Iva fretted that he would prove genetically incompatible to survive the tropics, too small, too fair, too white. She blurted this out to her mother as they pored over a caterer's brochure. Her mother reared up, pencil boring a hole alongside Triangular Sandwiches.

"Philip has a master's degree," she huffed, as if superior education were a prophylactic. "And besides, you will have screens."

This was true, a promise from Geneva. Mud and daub,

yes, but much improved upon. Cement floor, whitewashed walls, tin roof, a decent outhouse, good water. A lawn, they discovered when they arrived at the compound. And shutters. Not the long, thick, louvred variety of their florid hotel room, but small doors hinged to one side of openings in the walls. The openings, as promised, were covered with screens.

The shutters had been painted a sky blue. Iva kept them perpetually open. It was too hot otherwise. They wouldn't be able to sleep. But on certain nights, the Devil passed through the compound on his way into town. Then a man ran before him and banged on their door, shouting a warning. Philip and Iva would leap from their beds and latch each shutter tight.

Once, when Philip was off spraying, the entourage halted outside Iva's window. Musicians played while the Devil sang. Listening to this heart-stopping music, Iva wanted the Devil to know she only wished to be polite, that she had indeed made her window as sightless as possible. If the shutter didn't quite fit, this was not her doing, not done on purpose. She huddled under the netting, under the sheet, face turned toward the wall. The Devil is forbidden to the uninitiated. Like all expatriates, Iva had heard reports of people going home blind for supposed infractions. She knew these to be likely stories, tall tales, but ones she did not wish to test. The next morning, when their houseboy arrived, she brought up the subject of the Devil.

"He be angry, Missy, 'bout your shutters. They be open at night."

"But we can't possibly sleep with them closed. We'll suffocate."

Alfred shrugged. In this case, Iva's comfort was of no concern to him. Rules were rules, and some were infallible. Like Iva's directions for boiling water. Never less than five minutes—six, Iva warned Alfred as a precaution. She bought him a watch to count the time. He wore it proudly, always on display. At six minutes Alfred let the water cool before pouring it through a crockery filter into empty rum bottles. These he stored on a shelf in the door of their kerosene refrigerator, a greenish lineup of the redeemed.

Because the anopheles mosquito rested after each meal, Philip's task in Liberia was to direct his sprayers to cover the walls of every hut and farm shelter in a coloured zone on his map of Nimba County with DDT, and then to move on to the next shade. He returned from these expeditions reddened by heat and sun and, as the rains approached, by the bites of less harmful mosquitoes. He would remove his shirt and let Iva rub him down with witch hazel, then smooth on calamine. She would do this slowly, prolonging the contact. Let me help, she pleaded, make this easier for you. Certainly she could punch Surveillance Cards. Any moron could do that, she pointed out.

But Philip merely rose from the bed and replaced his shirt. Sometimes he put it on before the field of calamine dried into pink mud and cracked, and then a fleshy stain spread through the material. Iva had enough on her hands, he claimed, working the shirt's buttons. Running the house, he meant, as he kissed her companionably but did not linger. She watched him stride across the compound to his office. She saw the light go on, saw his head bend immediately to whatever littered his desk.

But he was wrong. Alfred ran the house. Alfred swept the floors and washed their clothes. Alfred even opened the tins of Danish hamburger and Argentinean corned beef. These he mixed with greens and served over rice. Once Iva carried her atlas into the kitchen to show Alfred the distance the tins had travelled to reach this house. She asked him to name the furthest he had ever gone and he replied, to the President's farm.

She came back with a pencil then and positioned two dots on a piece of paper, one for the malaria station and one for the President's farm. The dots stood side by side, touching. She opened her book to a map of the world. She pointed to Denmark and to Argentina, and to the map's scale. She wrote down figures, trying to estimate how many times Alfred would have to ride the money bus to the president's farm and back to reach these countries.

Alfred seemed delighted. His eyes widened. He oohed with wonder. He asked for the paper with the dots and her calculations. And could he have an empty can, the one with the picture of the cow? For his children, he said. He wanted them to be educated. He sent them to school. Every day. But, he sighed, there were problems.

He held a roll of leaves tight in his fist and lifted the knife, suspending it in the air. What problems? Iva asked, since this is what he waited for. What can I do?

Not enough teachers, Alfred replied as fine green strings strayed into the pot on his lap. The children wanted, he said. He gazed up sideways, craftily, at her.

The next morning Iva walked down the hill. The school's principal, a man with a welcoming gap, a way in through his front teeth, stood under his umbrella in the centre of the courtyard, supervising the raising of the flag. His wore a rigidly ironed khaki shirt and similar trousers, a feat, Iva recognized, in this climate. Her own dress hung limp and rumpled and was damp from her walk. She hoped its state would not be used against her. She asked the principal if she might help. She started giving him her credentials. He clapped his hands and laughed uproariously.

"Come this way," he said.

He took her to an unused hut just off the courtyard. Inside was a single large room, and here the youngest schoolchildren sat on wooden benches. The principal told Iva these children had to learn at least some English before they could be admitted to the first grade. No-one had time for them. He himself came for an hour a day but that was all he could spare because he also taught Grades 5 and 6. There were no books, he stated matter-of-factly, but there was a blackboard, which she could sometimes borrow.

"Just send the bigger boys for it," he said, leaving.

Iva faced four rows of eager faces. Girls in bright dresses, boys in shorts. Good morning, she began. The children knew these words. GOOD MORNING, they shouted back, GOOD MORNING, GOOD MORNING, GOOD MORNING. Iva waved her arms to quiet them. She felt herself a large white bird flown off course, ridiculous in this location. Suddenly a great noise filled the room. Rain pounded on the tin roof, the first real torrent of the season.

Iva had never heard such unyielding rain, but surprisingly the roof held. Yet something penetrated. Something that wasn't wet fell on her head and shoulders. Something more than just the clamour, this immense din. Iva stood still. She let her arms drop and shut her mouth. She waited. There could be no contest here. If a herd of elephants thundered through town, who would be foolish enough to stand in their way? She listened. She felt as if a magical sheet had been thrown round her, and she captured and carried off somewhere, not necessarily somewhere physical—she liked it well enough here in Liberia—but toward a territory of great improvement.

The children calmed too under this hail of rain. They smiled at Iva and giggled quietly at one another, content to be here, in this hut, on these hard benches, to not be home doing chores.

Iva walked to the door and opened it. The rain poured down, obliterating even the nearest houses. She wanted to shout with joy at the sheet of water streaming from the sky and off the roof. She stepped under the eaves and put out her hand. Cool rain pelted the soft skin on the inside of her forearm. Rivulets ran through the hollow at her elbow. She had prayed for such an outburst, had kept watch on the sky, waiting for any sign of the rains she hoped would cure that boiled look Philip had in the dries.

She had already tried once to fix it and failed. She had bought a fan in Monrovia, for their bedroom. But each night Philip, following Geneva's directions, following them explicitly, shut the compound's generator off at ten.

Sharp.

After 18 months in Liberia, the World Health Organization turned an eye toward Philip's future. They sent him across the continent, to the shores of Lake Victoria, to participate in a study on schistosomiasis. Schistosomiasis was right up Philip's alley. Like malaria, it needed a third party to be successful, in this case a snail. A person contracted

39

schistosomiasis by stepping into a body of water. It could be a huge lake or the smallest rain puddle, just so long as the fluke which transmitted the disease felt comfortable enough to drop out of the snail and swim about.

Philip told Iva he would need two weeks at Lake Victoria. She could spend the time in Nairobi. When he returned they would do the game parks. She told him about the rhino at Amboseli, about the photographs she had seen from aid workers, the animal posing, standing up right under Kilimanjaro. I want to see him, she told Philip, and he promised her they would.

On the airplane, Philip took the aisle seat.

"I have work to do," he said. "You enjoy the view."

The plane, a turboprop, lumbered slowly across the continent. Looking down, on jungle then savanna then jungle again, Iva wondered what the plane's shadow momentarily darkened, what animals, if any, stampeded in fear. She had hardly seen any of Africa's fabled creatures. Just some birds, and a pangolin, cowering in the arms of the boy who was selling it, and the pygmy hippos of the President's farm, the same President's farm of Alfred's travels. They merely stood bored and passive on their cement shoreline as their keepers washed down the pool. Far too complaint, too domesticated for Iva, hardly the stuff of legend. She desired bellows and trumpeting, pounding hooves and roars. On the way in from the airport she asked the taxi driver if lions still roamed the streets of Nairobi.

Philip chuckled at this. He gazed at the taxi driver's back, aligning himself with the man, African hands both. He told Iva not to worry, and put his pale hand on her thigh as if she had become excited.

"Lions won't venture in as far as our hotel," he said. "Am I right?" he asked.

In the rear view mirror Iva saw the driver's contemptuous smile.

"Madam," he said, "it is true lions do sometimes come into the city, but chances are slim. If you want to be frightened (How did he know?) go to the snake museum and see the python. He is as big around as a tree trunk and you will understand his pleasure in swallowing."

She went. The very day. Right after she waved Philip and his driver off. At the snake museum she found the python easily. The rest of the snakes lived in small boxes, behind glass windows. They draped themselves over sticks or lay coiled on their floors. But the python lived outside, in the central courtyard, in a real cage, the kind a lion would occupy, with a concrete pad and iron bars. It reclined down the middle like a fat insect queen, its body a glistening pampered tube. It was not as thick around as the trees of Iva's experience, but it remained impressive. She thought it beautiful and fascinating, immense power without arms and legs. She tried to imagine how it would feel to slide down its gullet, to be squeezed along by all that muscle. She wondered if it could see her and if so, if it imagined the same thing. She said this to the man who came and stood beside her. He laughed, a pleasant throaty companionable laugh. He introduced himself as Simon. He worked at the museum, he said. As apprentice expert.

He was taller than any of the Liberians Iva knew and a bit stout. His bigness pleased her, and also his upper lip, deeply puckered in the centre so that his mouth resembled a dark rose apple. He offered to show her around. She said she had two weeks to herself.

It turned out to be more like three. When Philip finally dragged himself away from Lake Victoria, he came upon Simon in his bed. Simon did not hurry off but took a lengthy shower while Iva packed and Philip held his bewildered ground, clutching his bag and briefcase as if they were railings to cling to.

"How could you?" he asked.

"We had no idea when you were coming, Philip."

It was a flippant answer, and cruel. But Iva had no urge to produce her other replies, the ones that truly explained the present circumstances. She was experiencing a most pleasant lethargy, the nicest amazement at just how little she felt for Philip at the moment. What few twinges managed to surface could be easily batted down using her new pleasures. She and Simon dancing. Simon driving her into the Ngong Hills to look down upon the Rift Valley. Simon and the river he knew of, massed with crocodile. The pair of them lying under a cone of thatch listening to buffalo pawing the earth.

"It's not a good time to talk, Philip," she said because some effort seemed required of her.

She made the empty hangers in the wardrobe clink above the noise of water streaming over Simon's body.

"We'll meet tomorrow. I'll come by."

Philip shot a glance at the hateful bed.

"You don't think I'm staying *here?*" he protested.

His complexion had reddened. So did hers now. A flush rose up her neck. But Iva was darker, almost olive. Her blushes were quite a bit more attractive. Previous boy-friends would provoke her just to bring them on. This was not the case with Philip's redness. His reminded one of a mishap, an ugly spill of hot water. Iva sighed. She was doing badly. She just wanted to be gone. She snapped the suitcase shut.

Just then Simon emerged from the bathroom, fully dressed. He nodded to Philip, marooned between bed and dresser, and went straight to the door.

"You forgot something," Philip said.

A man's shirt lay on the opened wardrobe's floor, a new shirt still in its wrapping, smugly folded. Iva picked it up. The cellophane packaging crackled like dry dead leaves.

"It's for Alfred," she said, holding the shirt toward Philip.

It had cost more than Iva intended to spend on Alfred but she couldn't resist. The shirt was covered in globes, the earth reduced to quarter-sized discs. She had wanted the pleasure of Alfred's reaction, his yellowed eyes looking sideways when he saw the pattern, his mouth curving in a faint smile. She knew he would remove the cellophane as slowly and noisily as possible and slip out the straight pins as if they were daggers in someone's back and he the investigating homicide detective. He would save everything, bring them home to his family, shake the shirt out again in front of them, lift his head with pride at the garment's deep creases, proclaiming the shirt's value as something new and shipped from far away.

"The earth in all its glory," Iva said, dropping the shirt on the unmade bed. "I'll send housekeeping up," she told him, as she ran into the bathroom to fetch her toothbrush before following Simon out the door.

Perhaps one of Alfred's children would write her a thank-you note. None arrived, and this left Iva pondering Philip's actions. That he had refused to give them an address. Possible. That he told Alfred *he* had bought the shirt. Unlikely and out of character—bear in mind the compound's generator—though he was welcome to the deceit, considering. Maybe the shirt never reached Liberia. Maybe Philip regarded the garment as contaminated by her touch, and had it destroyed, even incinerated to keep everyone safe. This she thought the most plausible of all. Iva did see Philip again, but never the shirt. She went back to the hotel as promised. The desk clerk stopped her as she started up the stairs, and gave her a new room number. The new room had a hopeful double bed, but no chairs. They sat on the mattress, at opposite corners.

"Come back with me," Philip said. "We'll try again."

He spoke in the same calm, deadly tone him used to mediate disputes between his sprayers. It made reconciliation sound inescapable. Iva was his partner in battle, he claimed in that modulated voice. They were a pair of St. Georges out to slay the dragon. And now there was a new enemy. Didn't she want to help?

She cut him off by rising and walking toward the door. The muscles of his face tightened now, like isometric exercises against his pain and hurt. He started up again, his voice running after her, describing the fluke's sharp spine, the blood that issued from a victim's bladder. As she wrenched the door open, he growled out a furious warning about faithfulness.

They did not speak again. Philip must have gone back to Liberia, because some weeks later Iva received a letter, forwarded in Philip's hand. The letter was from her mother,

43

rife with exclamation points as it praised Philip's devotion, his healing people even on his holiday. It proved a master-piece of clairvoyance. Unfolding the thick embossed pages, Iva came upon not one, but two clippings on the dutiful wife.

Simon rented a flat in a section of Nairobi once reserved for Asians. Linoleum covered all the floors, and the building itself looked like a motel. A cement walk ran down its length, front and back, and here the houseboys and the ayahs congregated in their spare time. There were no ser-vants quarters. To sleep, Simon's houseboy unfolded a can-vas cot in the flat's narrow galley kitchen. Simon planned to move. As soon as the museum let him lord it more over the snakes. All his friends were re-locating, to once lily-white suburbs. Houses there, he said, grinning broadly, were coming free at an alarming rate.

Simon revelled in his country's independence. He felt that the world was his and his friends' for the taking. He triumphed in the final rout of his colonial masters. The defeated English (as he saw them) were quitting the coun-tryside, getting the hell out and good riddance. Iva had heard the English described as rats deserting, but not by Simon, because for Simon the ship was only just streaming down the rails into the water, and champagne still dripped from its bow. His enthusiasm was proving infectious. Iva caught it willingly, found it sexy, certainly in contrast to Philip's morose plagues, mired still in dark jungle and no nearer to abatement. She gave herself ardently to Simon and his cause. She was puzzled when he quickly found her a flat of her own.

"Furnished," he mentioned caustically, as if the former owners had fled in panic.

This flat too had linoleum on all the floors, and a kitchen even smaller than Simon's. At night huge orange cock-roaches clambered over the walls there. Strangely, they never ventured into any other room, and by morning, when Iva rose, they had disappeared completely. Iva never saw them by daylight, even on the weekend when she was not working. She had found a job in a bank. The interviewing manager was only too happy to acquire her proficiency with English, combined with an ability to type (Kenyans with Iva's talents fell easily into more-elevated, higher-paying work) but he offered only a teller's wage. Take it or leave it.

Thereafter, Iva spent her days with the bank's correspondence. At noon she walked to the same lunch counter, and ordered their grilled cheese sandwich. It arrived reassuringly greasy and pressed flat. On Mondays she went from work to the central market for spaghetti makings. She cooked these into sauce, mixed in boiled pasta, and stuck the dish in the refrigerator. Roaches dislike the cold, she wrote her mother, adding a drawing, life-sized, she made sure she stressed, of one. On nights when Simon did not ask her out, she spooned dinner from this pot.

One day Simon left town for the weekend. He returned with a boy of six or seven, all elbows and knees, wearing shorts and a white shirt browned from the day's road dust.

"My son," Simon told her. Okoth, but Iva should call the boy, Thomas. "He doesn't speak English," Simon added, as Iva opened her mouth to greet the child.

They ate a silent dinner, *ugali*, corncake, with a beef sauce this time, and tapioca for dessert. Iva thought of pushing her bowl of tapioca across the table, for Thomas. The child seemed tense. His movements, plate to mouth, were jerky. He was either hungry or nervous or both. And Iva had lost her appetite, wondering through dinner what the boy's sudden appearance meant for her and Simon, if it meant something at all. But she didn't push her tapioca across the table, even though she didn't eat it herself. Simon had so completely ignored his son during the meal she felt she must do the same, that perhaps this was custom, and custom must be respected.

After supper Simon's houseboy bathed Thomas and put him to bed in the second bedroom. Iva went to say goodnight, even though Simon was repeating to her back, quite nastily, that the boy had no English. She hoped to defeat Simon here. If the boy would help her. If he would supply the word she needed, his word for goodnight, repeated back to him and understood. But Thomas lay silent and still, aware of her but refusing to acknowledge this, as if in doing so he would give himself away, surrender. He had folded his thin dark arms protectively over the blanket. She felt a rush of tenderness for this anonymous child, a kinship, another stranger, new to the city and at the mercy of Simon. She wondered how Thomas liked his new bed, the smooth sheets, the springs and mattress and pillow. Liberians slept on benches of hardened mud. What had Thomas slept on? And was his mother, at that very moment, kneeling beside the empty berth, keening at the injustice of it all?

"Listen," Iva whispered later, because the boy hummed.

She was lying under Simon. She could hear the boy on the other side of the wall. Simon only grunted with annoyance and thrust harder, but Iva kept one ear cocked. The humming went on and on but then it diminished, came only in spurts after longer and longer intervals. Finally it ceased entirely. The boy slept.

Simon enrolled his son at St. Michael's, a boarding school just outside Nairobi. For his new education, Thomas must dress in grey wool shorts and cap, and he must learn to knot a specific tie. These Simon purchased at a store on Kenyatta Avenue, which also sold tartan skirts and cable sweaters. Iva was sent elsewhere to buy Thomas's second tier, the underclothes and socks, the T-shirts and shorts he would need for play. Simon had pulled shilling notes from his wallet and told Iva where to go, which bus to take. She and Thomas alighted on a street lined with identical shops, the owners, in turbans and neatly folded beards, calling out to her as they passed, pointing to dresses hanging from the awnings, and to saucepans—Come buy, Madam—shiny as cut glass.

"You choose," she told the boy who wanted everything.

His first term ended just before Christmas. There was to be a Sport's Day and a tea for the parents, after which the boys went home. The evening before, Simon called Iva at the bank and suggested they eat out. He took her to a restaurant which doubled as a nightclub.

"One more dance," he kept insisting, dragging Iva onto

the floor.

They were the last patrons to leave. Normally Simon drove recklessly, but that night his car crawled through the darkened streets. When they reached his own neighbourhood, he became wary, peering into the blackness, flicking his eyes to the rear view mirror.

"Is something wrong?" Iva asked.

Simon shook his head. But once inside the flat he did not let her turn on any lights. She had to feel her way to the bathroom and undress in the dark.

They had just begun making love when a car drove up. Its headlights shone brightly through the thin curtains of Simon's bedroom. Iva thought the driver would soon notice his mistake and leave, but the car stayed. The motor died. The headlights stayed on.

Simon rolled off Iva, breathing heavily. He put a finger to her lips. The shouting began then.

"Let me in, Simon! I know you're in there! Open the door! OPEN THE DOOR!"

Whoever it was pounded on the outside wall. The window panes rattled.

"YOU FUCKER!" she shouted.

She drew closer. She neared the window. What would happen when she reached it? Would she shatter the glass, ploughing on through into the room, step over the shards to wreak her vengeance, Simon rising to come between them? A rush of warm conceit flooded Iva's body. To be the one lying here in Simon's bed; to *not* be the one outside, advertising her defeat. Iva's skin gleamed in the light pouring in through the window. Beside her, also lit, Simon's smoky testicles lay against his thigh, propping up his penis, its foreskin like a sleeve rolled down. She would like Simon to move up behind her, wrap her in his arms, have them face this woman together, in league. But instead he pulled the sheet up over Iva's head, and climbed across her body so that his own hid hers. She, his chosen one.

"Simon!" the woman wailed.

She had stopped in front of the window. She had halted her fists. She was not coming through. Iva could feel

47

Simon's body relax. He leaned backwards, his buttocks grazing her crotch, a hint that they would soon be making love again.

Iva pulled the sheet from her head. Her gloating slipped away then. It rose from the bed and crossed the room, peering out the window. It wanted a glimpse of this shouting woman. It left behind an odd melancholy, an apprehension that she, Iva, had been the one routed.

"Don't move," Simon whispered as if sensing her new mood.

Where would she go? Out onto the cement walkway to join this woman, the two of them pummelling the window in a duet, fists in unison, a double humiliation? No, not Iva. Iva lacked something this woman possessed. A certain critical lust. A necessary passion. Try as she might, Iva could not imagine herself outside any room, yelling to any man. Outside the gates of the snake museum, yelling at Simon. Outside the shed, Philip's office, Philip crouched over his endless surveys, Iva hollering to him to put down his damn hole punch, come across the lawn with her, reject his instructions for once, leave the generator to chug on all night.

She could not imagine ever making that much of a public spectacle of herself, even for love.

The woman's heels clicked on the pavement and grew faint. She was going, had given up, defeated by their callousness, and the sounds of neighbours roused. Her car door slammed. The motor started, the lights disappeared. The room was dark again.

Simon turned toward Iva. He cupped a breast and brought his lips toward hers. She pushed him away. She waited and when he said nothing, asked. Her name was Juliette, he answered flatly. They met a while back, before he met Iva. She taught school in Eldoret. Yes, he had known she was in town. He had known she would *be* in town because end-of-term was end-of-term for every school, not just for St. Michael's. Juliette's school, too, would have had a Sports Day and then shut down.

And...

his tone was mocking now,
by the way, (it seemed to her he said)...
he would soon be marrying yet a third woman, someone
from his tribe.

"Here's us, Philip. God, what an awful dress. A shift, no
less. What taste. And look at you, straight off the rack,
hardly time to pin up the cuffs. And Mother. So self-satis-
fied. How she hated me for letting her down."

"God rest her soul."

Iva grins. She places a finger on the next photograph, a
small boy in front of a red double-decker bus.

"This is Thomas," she tells Philip. "Simon's son."

"*Simon's* son?" Philip barks incredulously. "Simon sent
you a picture of his son?"

Iva grins again. She is enjoying this.

"Not likely," she says. "I took this picture."

It is many years later. Iva and Philip are both back in
Vancouver and Iva is showing Philip around her apartment.
They are standing in front of an arrangement of framed
photographs. Iva as a baby, hose in hand. Iva at her belated
graduation from university. Iva sporting long straight hair
and an apron, wielding a spatula, from her days as part-
time cook in a treatment centre for delinquent boys. Iva
and the potter she lived with at road's end, in Lund.
Thomas wearing a pair of long trousers.

"He came to live with Simon while I was still in Nairobi.
This is the day we went out to buy him clothes. Simon pro-
duced the money and told me where to go."

"And you went."

"Of course. It's what we girls did then. His first pair,"
she added, getting back to Thomas.

You decide, she told Philip she had told the boy, the
Sikh translating.

The child had wanted it all, of course. Everything the
Sikh had managed to cram inside his shop. You could see
the greed in his eyes, and in his excitement, suppressed
since Thomas was not a forthcoming child, not around her
anyway. But when the Sikh handed Thomas a pair of

49

trousers to try on, you knew the boy wanted these most of all. Because of how ceremoniously he lowered first one leg, then the other into the trousers' openings. Because of how formally he drew up the waist and pushed the button through the hole, and the careful pull he gave to the zipper. You knew because he gazed so longingly into the mirror Iva had demanded when they first entered the shop, the shopkeeper shouting into the back until someone came running in from the back, carrying the mirror out from behind a curtain.

The shop quieted. Everyone watched Thomas watching himself, witnessing the future, seeing his manhood. Iva bought him two pair. They shattered Simon's budget, and she had to shell out her own money for underwear and tennis shoes because these Simon expected. She posed Thomas in front of the bus on their way home. He was hugging a large parcel, wrapped in brown paper and tied with string, holding it up over his chest, high enough to give the camera a full view of his new long pants.

"His real name was Okoth," she tells Philip. "I wonder if he went back to using it."

Iva has invited Philip for dinner. He has arrived wearing a Harris tweed sport's coat over a pair of stiff jeans. Except for their wedding day, Iva had not seen him covered up this much in their whole marriage.

"Not *your* son then?" Philip makes her confirm.

Iva smiles.

"Don't be silly. I wasn't there that long."

His face freezes.

"I mean I wasn't there long enough to give birth and abandon."

Iva had been surprised, but not floored, to find Philip at her mother's funeral. For many years, Iva's mother had been writing Philip.

"He needs grounding, dear," she explained, unfolding his first reply, tapping the Ugandan postmark. "Look, he's moved on."

For two decades Iva's mother exposed Iva to Philip's

50

continuing life. It ran like a one-sided serial. Her mother never broadcast her own replies, but whenever a letter from Philip arrived she telephoned Iva and summoned her across the Lion's Gate Bridge. Iva would be led into her mother's sunlit living-room with its view across Georgia Strait and to avoid any distractions, be pointed to a wing chair that did not face the window. She would be handed a fork, a napkin, and a single slice of extremely plain cake. Then she would be read to. Philip had left Uganda for Bangladesh. He had moved on to Indonesia. He was back in Africa, in the Congo.

"That's Zaire, Mother," Iva corrected, wiping her mouth.

Her mother frowned. She turned her head away. A long pause ensued, a measure of Iva's disfavour. But eventually she returned to the page in her hand. Philip's letters were too good a hold over Iva to be put aside for any petty squabble.

He had a new assignment, in India. He had left India for Oxford to study something deadly.

"It's always deadly, Mother," Iva sighed that time. "Deadly is what turns Philip on."

"There's no need for sarcasm," her mother had sniffed in reply. "What exactly do *you* do for the world, Iva?"

(At this time, in the mid seventies, Iva had just returned to town from her hibernation with the potter. She was about to enter university for the third time, something her mother had grown tired of hearing. But this new course-work will lead to meaningful employment, as Iva enjoyed repeating to her mother over the years, in a job she still holds, at the forensics laboratory of the RCMP.)

"Philip is studying plague at Oxford," her mother resumed attack. "Did you even know there still was plague?"

And without waiting for an answer, she quoted the latest intelligence Philip so kindly supplied to her.

Iva endured these sessions by drifting off. She would invent the arrival of her mother's letters. She imagined them amongst the jumble accumulating at UN headquarters on some street in Kampala and Jakarta and Kinshasa, just as they had in Monrovia. In Oxford the envelope dropped

51

through an ancient mail slot landing heavily on a runner tattered by centuries of feet.

Or she would invent Philip receiving these letters. His last came from somewhere in Brazil. It bore a stamp exploding with flowers far bolder than those which clogged their Geneva hotel room. While her mother unfolded the pale blue air paper, meticulously cut so as not to lose a word, Iva imagined Philip going more native over the years, sleeping now on a raised platform, eating with his fingers. Philip had moved on from malaria. There were other afflictions to battle: dengue and yellow fever, leprosy and yaws. And the World Health Organization had given up on malaria. At least they gave up on spraying. It could not be properly monitored and it proved useless once the anopheles mutated. The anopheles was already mutating when Iva met Simon in Nairobi. To Simon the mosquito's resistance matched that of Mau Mau. Or the partisans of that day, the North Vietnamese. To Simon the mosquito was proving satisfyingly clever, outwitting Philip and every other white.

In Iva's drifting, Philip's mail arrives by dugout canoe. To a thatch house on poles, Philip sitting cross-legged on a mat. A pet boa lies nearby. The boa is Philip's revenge on Simon. It lifts its muscular head with interest at the well-heeled envelope in Philip's hand. It slithers over.

Just dear old Iva's mother, Philip tells the boa. Not a very satiating meal. Too little meat. Here, this is better.

And Philip serves the boa what? A mongoose, a tapir, a rat?

Philip chortled when Iva told him this. He slapped his side with pleasure until Iva feared he would fall over from the force, or a least make a decent welt. He was still so slight. He must be one of the world's few men who would actually benefit from a small paunch. At the funeral, he slipped easily into a pew at the back of the church. She hadn't seen him until after the service, when he came up to her in the condolence line. Despite the occasion, he could not help grinning at her surprise. He told her he had read the obituary in the newspaper. He had just moved back, he said, having been blacklisted. Dysentery. Forty pounds in a weekend. A colleague had driven him miles to a hospital where they punctured veins in both his arms and turned the stopcocks on full to replenish him.

The dysentery had made Philip susceptible to other ailments. Malaria, he admitted sheepishly. They sent him home. He was at Simon Fraser.

"Those who can't, teach," he said, attempting a joke.

He offered to help Iva dispose of her mother's ashes. He drove her, the next weekend, to Horseshoe Bay. They went down to the docks and hired a boat. Clouds hung low and rain threatened. The rental agent kept looking from them to the sky, but they took no notice.

Philip aimed the boat for the back of Bowen Island. He cut the motor when he and Iva were too far off shore to be seen with the naked eye, and when, for the moment, there were no other boats about.

"Just wait a minute," he said as Iva began untying the ribbon.

He reached inside his backpack. He brought forth a half bottle of champagne, and two glasses wrapped in soft cloths. Iva raised her eyebrows. She was remembering the compound's generator. Not only was this expedition illegal, but just a short time before Philip had signed the boat's rental agreement without hesitation, directly under the words: No alcohol on board.

The cork flew into the water. The liquid fizzed. Iva undid the cardboard box. It was a perfect cube, fitting, she felt, for her mother, with its sharp corners and equal sides, its complete order. She leaned over and tilted its contents into the dark sea. The ashes sank quickly, more quickly than she had anticipated, and she had a moment of panic. She had counted on time for a few brief words. She had practised a rapid farewell. Her mother would have expected to be dispatched with at least some ceremony.

Grateful, Iva watched the ashes halt, as if reaching a certain point in their journey, an agreed upon meeting place. They seemed to wait now for everyone to catch up. Quickly Iva mumbled her short speech, and then the ashes, as if still connected, still an entity, still a body, washed in a single pale, yellowish wave under the boat and out to sea.

Philip poured the champagne. Together they lifted their glasses and saluted the fluid path they perceived Iva's mother to be taking. Iva hoped the tide was right, that her mother was not rushing back toward shore to be washed up on the rocks. She knew who would be blamed for that fiasco. She poured the champagne down her gullet, where it rolled once round her stomach before going straight to her head. She turned her gaze on Philip. It was drizzling now, a steady soft mist. Perhaps it was the rain, or the light—maybe the malaria, although malaria should make one yellow—but Philip looked like he had darkened over the years, as if his dogged redness had been replaced by a wiser colour. And there were spots on his hand which Iva found pleasing. She started counting them for something to focus on. Brown age spots, most likely, but she had reached the point when imperfections became reassuring. The spots gave Philip an effervescence. Like the champagne Iva was throwing back. They bubbled off his deadly earnestness, the humourless determination he once shared with army ants, relentless columns he stepped across in his treks through the bush.

A dish towel hangs over Iva's shoulder. She has a wooden spoon in her hand. She has promised Philip a groundnut stew for dinner. Just like Alfred's, or almost.

"He must have been quite lonely, that poor boy," she says of Thomas, moving down the hall.

She knows she should stop, switch to another topic, but she cannot help herself.

"He used to sing himself to sleep."

She hums tunelessly as she enters the kitchen. It smells of peanut butter and rice. She holds up a plastic tub.

"Not exactly authentic, not pounded in a mortar"—and she imitates the Liberian women with their life-sized pestles, rhythmically mashing nuts or husking rice. "But good. A glass of wine, Philip?"

He doesn't answer.

54

"Sit down, why don't you?" she suggests.

But Philip remains in the doorway. He is glaring at her. The glare feels good to Iva. She raises her head to it, as if to the sun. The redness is creeping back up Philip's neck.

"Would it help, Philip, if I told you that I too was supplanted. Overthrown. That Simon married from under me, so to speak."

"That's disgusting," he says.

He has finally moved closer. He is tightening a fist around papers he brought with him. Iva suspects that Philip planned to sit in a chair in her living-room and read these pages peacefully while she finished cooking them dinner. The papers crackle as he closes his hand. She has the absurd desire to take the dish towel from her shoulder and wave it between them like a bullfighter's cape.

"You are not the mother of this Thomas?" he repeats.

"I am not. Don't you think he looks a bit dark for that?"

She has taken up a knife and is cutting the stalks from a pile of collard greens.

"Then who is?" Philip bites off.

"Simon's country wife."

"Simon's *country wife?*" Philip yelps, as if someone has just stepped on his foot.

"That's what they called her."

"And what were you? His city wife."

"Or his naive wife. Just one of many."

"One of many!"

She pushes the collard stalks to one side and gathers up the leaves, which now all have a V-shaped notch.

"Well, there was also Juliette, his "English" wife. That's in quotes, Philip. Juliette was a teacher. And then there was the woman Simon actually married, or least told me he would. Someone from his tribe, but she was *not* Thomas's mother. And God knows who came after her. You were right about faithfulness, Philip."

"And where was this mother of Thomas while you were fucking her husband," Philip shouts, losing control.

"While he was fucking me, you mean."

She has stacked the greens on the cutting board, just like

Alfred used to do, with the largest leaf at the bottom to use as wrapping.

"Actually, she wasn't far from where you were, Philip," she tells him, rolling the leaves tight. "With your schistosomiasis."

He has the decency to tone down his glare a bit.

"Somewhere near the lake," she adds, picking up the knife again and slicing. Her ribbons have never been as fine as Alfred's. She doesn't have the patience.

"The polygamous bastard," he begins again, but more contritely.

"Simon is dead, Philip."

That quiets him.

"I didn't know," he finally blurts out.

"How could you?"

Philip is standing in the middle of the room. The air in his lungs comes out in a rush, as if he had been holding it there for ransom, and negotiations are now complete. A moment before, at the height of his anger, his free hand, the one without papers, had been rising toward Iva. It drops now, unneeded. Not that he could have reached her from where he stood. Not that he would actually have struck her if he moved into range. But the rising hand remained a gesture worthy of note, almost admirable considering.

Iva puts down her knife and walks toward Philip. She takes the spent hand and completes his original motion, bringing his palm to her cheek. And then to her lips.

On the stove a pot boils over, hissing and spitting.

"A message from the other side," she whispers, and lets go the hand to attend it.

Montana

Dave Margoshes

When he was 10 or 11, the pressure cooker of his hormones just starting to simmer, Frankie ran away from home, lighting out for the West—Montana, he hoped—and got as far as Pennsylvania, he thought, spending two nights on his own before being picked up by the police and brought home.

It wasn't the first time he'd run away, or been brought home by a policeman.

When he was 9, for instance, the copper who picked him up at Coney Island, where he'd gone by subway hoping to run off to sea on a tramp steamer, called him a "dumb nigger" but later made up for it by buying him a frozen custard while they waited for his father to come home and answer the phone.

"Don't be stupid," a social worker at the station told the cop, but he just shrugged his big Irish shoulders and went out to get the cone.

"I ain't no nigger," Frankie sulked, and the social worker laughed. "You're right, but don't say ain't." She laughed again, but she was frowning, too.

Another time, another police station, to help him while the time away, another cop had given him paper and pencil to draw with. Instead, he began to write about the horse he knew he'd have some day. "That's not bad," the cop said, looking over his shoulder. "Why don'tcha write a letter to your dad, tell him you're sorry for running away."

"I'm not," Frankie said, but he obediently set pencil to paper. "Dear Poppy," he wrote, "I'm sorry I ran away again."

This time, he meant not to get caught. He had a plan, some money, more nerve. All that worked and he was miles away, out of the city and short-hopping through New Jersey before lunch time. Later in the day, he got a ride from a friendly man in a Cadillac and had an adventure he more or less forgot about in later years—forgot about the whole thing, really: the running away, the plan, Montana, the man in the Caddy, what happened afterwards, sleeping in a hobo shanty the second night, getting picked up by the state police the third day, *letting* himself get picked up.

More than 20 years later, and just a year before the automobile accident that took his life, Frankie, calling himself François Stern now, found himself in Montana for the first time. It was the first time he'd been back in the States since fleeing to Canada a few years earlier, when the whole world had seemed to be falling apart after Nixon sent the bombers into Cambodia. He'd been involved in something in Ames, Iowa, that had gotten out of hand and he'd thought he was a fugitive, and maybe he was, so he was nervous at the border, but the customs man, the holstered pistol belted high on his waist, barely gave him a glance in the back seat of Dave's car. He'd been in Canada long enough to be legal and his ID was good, but no-one ever asked to see it.

His friends Dave and Ilya had a cabin at a place near St. Mary, a village just outside Glacier National Park where the road leading over the mountains and the Continental Divide is called Going to the Sun Highway.

Frankie found himself drinking strong coffee at a picnic table in the sun on a deck looking out over a lake called Lower St. Mary and rolling both those phrases around in his mind: *continental divide, going to the sun.* "The address here is Deck, Cabin, Stone's Throw from Lake, Montana," Dave said. "Don't know the postal code. In case you were wondering where you were."

"I usually am," Frankie said.

Then Dave and Ilya went for a walk, leaving Frankie alone. As he often did those days, he soon was thinking about his father, who had suffered a stroke a few months earlier and was only partly recovered. There was a portable typewriter inside and he lugged it out and set it up on the picnic table, which had peeling blue paint and knife scars across its top, making it look like one of those high altitude aerial photos of Vietnam after a bombing run. He meant to write his father a letter.

From where he sat, he could see the lake, long but narrow, and the opposite shore, which was fringed with some sort of evergreens. Behind them was a road, the highway they'd come down on from Calgary, where he'd been living the past few months, and behind the road there was an open meadow sloping up toward a thin belt of some kind of brush and then a dense forest of evergreens again that appeared to be as high as the upper half of his thumb, viewed with his arm extended. The whole thing was level at the top, making it more like what's called a ridge than a mountain, he supposed. To see real mountains, the kind with pointy crests and massive sloping shoulders, he'd have had to get up and walk down to the beach, looking south or to the west, behind the stand of poplars bordering the cabin. On the drive down, he'd seen some of them, mountains that looked like something on a postcard from Italy or Switzerland—massive and blue, a discoloured tooth in the open mouth of some fearsome giant. There was something frightening about them.

"What you're supposed to feel, I know, is *awe*," he had told Dave and Ilya, "because you're reminded of the majesty and power of nature and the insignificance of man, on the scale of things. That sort of thing."

"And you don't?" Ilya asked. She was a slim, dark-haired woman who reminded him vaguely of his cousin Becky, whom he hadn't seen in years.

"Nothing like that. What I feel is the same sort of tightening in the pit of the stomach you get when you turn a dark corner and the street ahead of you is completely empty—no shoppers, no cars, no lighted windows—except for three big guys walking shoulder to shoulder down the sidewalk toward you, like a tidal wave about to engulf you and half the world beside."

59

They'd all laughed at the intensity of Frankie's description and he'd soon forgotten about it. Just the same, he'd passed up joining his friends for a walk to the high meadow behind the cabin, where the mountains would leer down all around them. And from where he was sitting now, his vision focused on the gentle blue undulation of water and sky, the feeling seeping through his veins was more one of peacefulness than dread.

The previous evening, after a chili supper, they'd gone for a short stroll along the beach, which was covered with a foot-trapping mixture of sand and small stones and all sorts of greenery he didn't know names for. Ilya pointed some of them out and he tried to remember those names now, something to catalogue in his letter. There was a red-osier dogwood directly in front of him, its branches spilling over onto the deck, and, to his right, a little birch, and, just past it, an alder which he had thought must be a cherry because of the white markings on the smooth dark bark. All around the deck and cabin stood massive cottonwoods, their branchless trunks huge arrows pointing toward the sky, and slender girl-like aspens, their leaves trembling like scarves and hearts, and just before the beach, a spruce, its flanks bristly as a three-day beard. It surprised him, considering he had once cut trees down for a living and would know a lodgepole pine or a black spruce anywhere, even in the dark, how little he knew about trees, plants in general, the outdoors.

He rolled a sheet of paper into the machine and began to type, starting off by describing the scene, he way he used to do when he would write imaginary letters to his father in his head. "All of these things I've been mentioning are called *trees*," he wrote, "that's what they are, different types of trees. I mention that because I know, while you've never seen anything like these, you probably have heard of trees, perhaps have even seen one or two, in a park or a museum."

He pulled the page out of the typewriter, crumpled it and rolled in a fresh sheet. "Dear Pops," he wrote, though he knew that might annoy the old man. "Guess where I am? Montana, of all place. I'm visiting some friends, at a cabin on a lake. My hosts have gone off to pick berries my hostess promised to bake into a pie for me this evening, and left me here with the typewriter, the picnic table, the deck, the trees, the lake—and you, somewhere over there, far behind that ridge, way out of reach."

He had been thinking all morning, and the day before, as they'd driven down through the brown, rolling Alberta hills, and when they'd crossed the border and the green and brown mountains began to open up ahead of them, that he was here, finally, that he had finally made it to Montana.

"Do you remember how I used to talk about going to Montana and having a sheep ranch?" he wrote. "Having one or working on one, I don't remember. God only knows where I got the idea, or how I knew they raised sheep here. You used to call me the little Basque sheepherder, remember that? I remember I thought it would be quiet—sitting in the mountains, watching the sheep eat grass—and I could think. There was always such a racket at home in those days, people coming and going, all your committees and political work, there wasn't any place I could get away from it."

When Frankie had asked about sheep, Dave said he thought there were some in the state, but further to the east, where it's flatter, more like prairie. They'd seen huge herds of cattle grazing on the brown, sloping meadows as they drove south, strikingly different terrain than that of his boyhood daydreams, in which he had always seen himself riding a horse through flocks of sheep stretching out before him like a white sea, with high, straight pine trees and brooks all around him, and snow-capped peaks of mountains in the not-very-distant distance.

"I used to think about it a lot, and talk about it a lot, too," he typed out. "It must have been the sound of the word, *Montana*, that Spanish sweetness on the tongue, that attracted me, that and the incredible distance—to me, it wasn't a real place at all, but a magical, mythical place of possibility, a Camelot. But I had forgotten all about it, that childhood daydream, I mean, not the actual state itself— and this is weird, in all the travelling I've done, back and forth across this country, hitchhiking and in buses and trains, I think there's only half a dozen states I haven't been in, but Montana is one of them, like fate was saving it for me, for the right time. Forgotten, I swear, until yesterday, when we were driving down and the word *Montana* kept coming up, flying around the interior of the car like a moth batting itself against the windows trying to get out, and suddenly it caught hold in one ear and clicked—Montana! Oh, you mean we're going to *Montana*."

Then it had all come flooding back.

Not just the shepherding daydream, but the running away, the heading out after it.

"It was gone completely from my memory," he typed, "and now it's back, bingo, just like that, almost as if it had happened last week, some of it anyway. I remember I wrote you a letter from a sort of railroad shack in New Jersey where I spent a night and almost froze my ass off, and I remember the New Jersey state police picked me up and brought me home."

Actually, the state policeman had taken him to the Holland Tunnel and turned him over to a Port Authority policeman, who'd driven him through the tunnel and turned him over yet again, to a city cop who brought him home. He remembered the Jersey trooper because he got to ride in the front seat of his car, the radio crackling, all the way from Cherry Hill, where he was picked up, to the tunnel, a couple hours' drive, and he listened to the police radio and thought that was kind of cool, even though he didn't like cops any better in those days than he did now. He remembered the Jersey cop as being pretty decent, though.

"I remember he talked to me like I was a real person, a human being," Frankie wrote, "and we stopped somewhere on the highway and he bought me something to eat and a cup of coffee. That's the thing I remember best about him —that he bought me a coffee without batting an eyelash, without asking if I was allowed. We went into a diner and sat down at the red formica counter with the truckers and he ordered two coffees, just like that. I'd already been drinking coffee for a while—you never cared one way or another—so it wasn't like it was any great treat or anything. I was just impressed with the way he did it."

He had been thinking all morning about that runaway trip because he had a feeling that he had learned something then that he'd forgotten, just as he'd forgotten the runaway itself, just as he'd forgotten Montana, and that it was something of value, something he ought to know, now. "In the strange way that fate works, it's almost as if things conspired to bring me down here," he wrote his father. "Writing the sonata, having it performed in Calgary, the university job, making friends with these people, them inviting me down here this weekend."

He stopped to light a cigarette—"did you know that I'm smoking again, or that I'd quit?" he thought, addressing himself to his father, but he didn't bother to type that— and pace around on the deck. He sat at the picnic table again, one leg curled under him, smoking and watching the lake. A wind had come up and the water was moving in lazy curls toward the north, whitecaps breaking occasionally through the rippled blue like little tongues. A yellow canoe was overturned on the beach and Dave had said perhaps they'd go out in it later, but the lake didn't look very inviting now. The night before, when they walked on the beach in the pale moonlight, the lake had been like glass at their feet, smooth, shimmering, silent. Now it was making a chopping noise along the shore, like a heavy rain.

"Things change here quickly, unexpectedly," he typed. "All morning, Ilya was trying to find some kind of bird to show me, a certain type of bluebird peculiar to the mountains, but one would not appear. Now, since I've lit this cigarette, two bright blue blurs have flickered by and one is perched on the little birch by the steps—or is that an alder? —singing at me. I know you can't see, can't hear, but perhaps you can remember hearing of such things in your youth, of birds and of singing."

He kept going over that runaway trip in his mind, turning it over and over, looking for something, amazed at how well he could remember it—and new pieces, like chips from a broken vase, kept surfacing, falling into place—as if the whole thing was seared into his memory like the brands he'd seen on the flanks of cattle alongside the road the previous day—although, funny, he couldn't remember if he was gone for two days or three.

"I left one day," he typed, "April or May, maybe, and I don't remember specifically why—maybe you do—but I was sore about something and determined to really do it. I had run away a couple of times before, and when I came home you always seemed almost indifferent, as if you'd been just as glad to be rid of me, which is something I always believed, true or not. But this one was going to be different. I wasn't going to chicken out and come back, I was going to make it out to Montana, get a job on a sheep ranch as a herder or whatever they do, and...well, I don't know what else. I must have had some idea then, but if I did I've forgotten it. As you can see, I don't remember *everything*."

He hadn't known about bindles, and didn't have a bandanna, anyway, so he stuffed a few things into a paper bag along with three peanut butter sandwiches wrapped in wax paper and an apple, put that under his arm and walked across town and took a bus up to the George Washington Bridge. He had a few bucks that he'd scooped up from the cookie jar in the kitchen where his father kept change, and a $10 bill he'd found on his father's dresser one day months before and hid away for a rainy day.

He had thought he'd take a bus across the bridge and start hitching in New Jersey but they cost more than he wanted to pay so he stood on one of the curving ramps leading up to the bridge with his thumb sticking out and someone picked him up right away, a woman with bundles piled all over the back seat. Of course, he lied—a 10-year-old couldn't say he was running *away* from home, he had to say he was going back. Frankie had figured it all out beforehand, and that's what he told people all that day as he moved west and south through New Jersey—that he'd run away, gone to the city, but had changed his mind and was heading home.

It worked great—people smiled at him, told him what a sensible boy he was and didn't give him any lectures. One man even gave him a $5 bill. He had to keep the rides short, though—he quickly figured out that if he said he was going to a place the drivers were going, they'd want to take him right to the door; and if it was a town further than theirs, they might want to drop him off at the police in their town. He had to quickly figure out where they were going, then name a town before that, so he'd be left off on the highway, at the outskirts. He didn't know any of those places, of course, but he memorized the names of towns and their distances apart from the road signs. Remembering it, more than 20 years later, it seemed hopelessly complicated to Frankie, beyond the abilities of a 10-year-old, but it hadn't seemed that way then, and it worked. He'd wave goodbye to those nice people, then stick his thumb out again as soon as they were out of sight. He had a lot of short rides and it took him most of the day to get across New Jersey, but they came one after another with no long waits, no hassles. A couple of times, he spotted a police car and dove into the bushes.

He'd just done that, and was coming out of the bushes, when he got his last ride of the day, from a small white-haired man in dark glasses, driving a pale blue Cadillac. He was quite sure he had seen the Caddy drive past a few minutes earlier.

"No, you're not," the skinny driver said as soon as Frankie started to spill out his story. "Don't make me laugh. You are *so* running away." He swivelled his head toward him and puckered his lips into a kind of frown that caused his glasses, which had bright tortoise-shell frames, to slide forward on his nose, almost toppling off. Frankie had already had nine or ten rides, and this man was the first one to see through his story, and it surprised him, but there was nothing menacing about the man, who looked like a drawing of Ichabod Crane in a book at school. Even his frown was only half-hearted.

"Where are you really from? New York?"

"Yeah." Frankie had the feeling he wouldn't be able to

lie to this man, so he didn't try.

"Uh huh. And heading west, no doubt." The man had already looked Frankie up and down several times, his eyes dark and sly beneath snowy white brows, but he gave him a quick once-over again, smiling a little at the pointy tips of his boots—cowboy boots his father had given him, along with a pair of jingly spurs, for Christmas after Frankie begged and pleaded—sticking out under the folded cuffs of his jeans. "To be a cowboy?"

"Not exactly," Frankie said. Without making a conscious decision about it, he suddenly trusted the Caddy driver. He told him about Montana.

"Sheep, huh?" He smiled and made his eyes roll up, the way Frankie had seen Milton Berle do the couple of times he and his father had gone across the hall to their neighbour's place to watch TV. Frankie laughed. The man was wearing a blond tweed sports jacket with leather patches at the elbow and powder blue slacks, almost the colour of the Caddy, with a razor sharp crease. Tufts of milky white hair poked out from beneath a matching tweed cap and a dark blue scarf was wrapped around his neck. He looked like a slightly dissipated version of a grandfather on a *Saturday Evening Post* cover, someone old enough to have used up all his violence and meanness but not so old the cunning's been ground out of him, a man who likes to take small boys fishing and impress them with his skill in putting worm to hook. "And you had a fight with your folks, I suppose."

"I don't have any *folks*," Frankie said. "Just a father. And there wasn't any fight." What he had done, though he couldn't have put it into words, was quit trying to bear it.

"Ran out of steam, eh?" The man looked at him over his sliding glasses and Frankie felt like he knew exactly what he meant. There didn't seem to be any point in lying to him, nor to tell him anything, either, because he already knew.

They drove along for a while, talking a little, and Frankie loosened up and cozied against the window, his head bouncing against the glass. They grinned at each other as they passed by the town Frankie had said he was going home to. The telephone poles racing past them outside ran into a blur and the Caddy hummed like a cat being stroked. It was painted to the highway, it ran so smoothly, and it was cool inside, like the lobby of a movie theatre, a relief after the heat of the sun outside. Frankie was certain they crossed a bridge into Pennsylvania, but then he slept a little and the next thing he knew it was dark and the Caddy was slowing down, stopping.

"Where are we?" He had been hoping to see the Pennsylvania Dutch country, which one of the kids at school had talked about during a show and tell, and now he was sure, suddenly, that he'd missed it.

"We're stopping for supper. Hungry, aren't you? Your stomach's been singing to me for a while."

The peanut butter sandwiches had long been eaten, and he was ravenous and wide awake. He had no idea where they were—no sense of city or country—but they had pulled up along a driveway lined with crushed stones to a magnificent white building fronted with arches and pillars and surrounded by dense shrubbery highlighted by hidden lights. The Caddy stopped beneath a canopy that seemed to be fluttering in a light breeze and a black man dressed like a general in a movie about Napoleon Frankie had seen at the Apollo was coming through a broad double glass door and down a set of low stairs toward them. Behind him, the windows of what appeared to be the lobby of a hotel glittered and Frankie could see smart-looking people moving about with grace and dignity. He pressed his nose to the Caddy's window until the doorman swung it away from him and he realized with a start that he was the first Negro he'd seen since getting off the bus at the George Washington Bridge that morning. He hadn't thought anything about it.

They went into the lobby and his friend took him by the hand in a proprietary way. Frankie had only seen him seated until then, and he'd had the sense of him being a small man, so he was surprised by how tall he actually was, almost as tall as his father, and how limber. Despite his white hair and lined face and the almost comical way his glasses rode along his lengthy nose, he moved with precision and grace, easily, like an athlete. His hand, Frankie noticed, was cool.

The only hotel Frankie had ever seen was the Theresa, on Amsterdam Avenue, and it was nothing like this. His eyes were wide as they walked through the lobby toward the front desk, past furniture that seemed to be made of thick, cream-coloured clouds. A woman with enormous blue eyes and wearing a long silvery blue dress with a scooped neckline was standing at the desk, chatting with the clerk behind it, and she smiled at Frankie, an amused, delighted smile, as if she had never seen a 10-year-old boy in dungarees and cowboy boots in a hotel lobby before and was relishing the idea.

"Is Mr. Faust around and about?" the Cadillac man asked the clerk, taking off his cap and nodding his head in the direction of the woman. His blowsy white hair formed a peak at the top of his head and he ran a hand through it, patting it down.

The clerk was a skinny boy with a large Adam's apple and pimples not very well concealed beneath caked ointment. He pulled his eyes reluctantly away from the woman in the long dress. "Sure," he said diffidently.

"Tell him Mr. Polite is here."

Frankie let himself be led to a sofa within sight of the desk and they dropped onto cushions that threatened to engulf him. The clerk stood behind the desk hesitating until the woman, leaning forward, whispered in his ear, laughed and walked away. Then he disappeared behind a partition. Frankie let his eyes follow the woman, who was absolutely the most beautiful creature he'd ever seen, until she was lost from view down a short flight of carpeted steps and behind a pillar, then kept himself busy examining the plush lobby furniture, the potted plants and the rich carpets, so he didn't see the clerk re-emerge, nor did he see the extremely fat man until he was upon them.

"Mr. Polite! What have we here?"

The Caddy man got up grinning, his hand extended. "Have someone here I'd like for you to meet, Mr. Faust.

68

Frankie, say hello to my good friend, Mr. Faust, who is going to be, I certainly hope, our host for dinner."

The man who stood towering above Frankie was hugely, monstrously, grotesquely fat, but there was, oddly, nothing menacing about him, just as there had been no apparent sense of danger about the man in the Cadillac. Frankie was sure he'd never seen anyone even nearly as fat and he was, simultaneously, repelled, amused and fascinated. He was still seated in the deep cushions and the man stood so close to him that his belly, dressed in the thin, whitish material of a seersucker suit, seemed to loom even larger than it really was, all but obscuring his upper body and face. Frankie scrunched back into the sofa, as far from that floating white balloon of fat as he could get, but, at the same time, he wanted mightily to stick his finger into it, to see how far it would go, the way you stick a finger into rising dough to see if it's ready for the oven. He did not say hello, as he'd been commanded, or anything else.

"Well, hello there, boy," a voice boomed down at him from somewhere north of that giant belly. "Frankie, is it? Welcome, Frankie, most pleased to meet you." A huge, soft-looking hand, white and puffy like the gloved paws of Mickey Mouse and Bugs Bunny, descended and waved in front of Frankie's face. He stared at it dumbly.

"I think the boy is impressed, *most* impressed with you, Mr. Faust," the Caddy man said.

"I believe you're right, Mr. Polite." The hand withdrew, and the belly retreated by perhaps a foot, giving Frankie breathing room. He wriggled to his feet and looked around. To his left, around the obstacle of the fat man, was the front desk, where the Adam's apple of the skinny clerk floated like a buoy in a sheltered pocket of water, his runny eyes casting nervously in their direction above the pimples. To Frankie's right, past the powder blue knees of his companion, was the double-doored entranceway through which they had come. He was not considering bolting, but he felt more comfortable on his feet, knowing the lay of the land.

"The boy is terribly hungry," the man called Mr. Polite said. "And I could do with a bite to eat myself." The white brows above his eyes arched like caterpillars stretching themselves in the sun. "And he is tired, too, the dear boy. He's been travelling all day long and has come a long way. And the same for me, I might add." He got up suddenly, his long, lean legs raising his body effortlessly, like a pneumatic jack. "I had hoped, Mr. Faust, that we might be able to avail ourselves of some of your deservedly famous hospitality."

The fat man beamed, his face breaking into a patchwork of thick lines and folds, his lips parting to reveal teeth large as kernels of candy corn. "Of course, of course. How rude of me not to have offered immediately. I'll see that something is prepared at once." He put a puffy hand on Frankie's shoulder. It felt soft and weightless, as if it were a balloon. His voice dropped, almost to a whisper. "Are we not being a bit indiscreet, however, Mr. Polite?"

"Not at all, Mr. Faust." The Caddy man laced his fingers together and pushed the palms away from him. He raised his voice. "My nephew and I will be delighted to join you for a late snack. How gracious of you to offer. Come along, Frankie."

Frankie *was* hungry, and very tired, and he let himself be led along. He registered Mr. Polite's reference to him as his nephew, but it didn't alarm him and he didn't question it.

The fat man stopped to quietly say something to the desk clerk and then they were standing before the ornate brass doors of the elevator. An ancient mulatto with a toothless grin and cheeks wrinkled as a roasted turkey's skin sat on a low stool inside the elevator. He gave Frankie a sharp glance. "Seventh floor, Mr. Faust?" he asked cheerfully.

"That is correct, Charles," the fat man said. His voice was elegant but weary, as if he had engaged in this particular exchange hundreds, perhaps thousands, of times and was bored with it. As the door slid closed, Frankie could see the woman in the long dress resume her position at the front desk, waving a gloved hand gaily at them.

The elevator creaked and moved slowly upward. There were no electric numbers to indicate the floors, but Frankie could actually see them through the grating of the folding door as they rose past. At a few of the landings, he caught glimpses of faces through the glass triangles of the outer doors, but the elevator didn't stop. No-one said anything until the elevator slowed and came to a jerking halt. "Here we is, Mr. Faust," the ancient man said, folding open the inner door.

"Ah," said Mr. Faust. They stepped out into a long carpeted hallway lined with closed doors. A cart with the ruined remains of someone's dinner on it sat beside one door, a soiled napkin hanging listlessly from the handle. Mr. Faust shook his head disapprovingly and led Frankie and Mr. Polite down the corridor. Behind them, the elevator began its creaking descent.

At the end of the hall, there was another elevator behind a door barely wide enough for Mr. Faust to squeeze through. It was marked "private." He inserted a key and the door instantly slid open. He waved the others in ahead of him, then cautiously negotiated his own way in, scrunching up his shoulders and laughing an embarrassed titter. The elevator was tiny, but padded with velvet quilting. The ceiling was a mirror. Mr. Faust pushed a button and the door slid silently closed, the elevator slid silently up. Frankie couldn't actually feel it move, but the door opened again and they were on a different floor, stepping out into a dimly lit foyer lined with mirrors and leading to a carved wooden door. Mr. Faust opened the door with a key. "Welcome to my humble home, gentlemen," he said grandly.

"Ah," said Mr. Polite. "At last. I'm famished."

"There will be just a short wait," Mr. Faust said. "Please, make yourselves at home."

Nothing in his short life had prepared Frankie for the opulence and mystery of the hotel. Mr. Faust, despite his great size and elegant way of speaking, was just another person, not so much strange as *different*, which was a quality Frankie liked and admired. So was Mr. Polite, different, and pleasantly so. But the hotel, with its doorman and desk clerk and elevator operator, its lobby and plush sofas, its carpets and mirrors and carts, its elevators and women in long dresses, was more than just different, it was totally beyond his experience, another world.

The apartment Mr. Faust led them into was the most elegant thing Frankie had ever seen. The foyer opened onto a living-room/dining-room combination, an open gleaming kitchen at the far end separated from the main area by a long floating countertop lined with open-back stools. The creamy white walls were thick with framed paintings and photographs; large drape-lined windows dominated one side of the living-room, a fireplace made of pink, irregularly shaped stones the other. The apartment was cluttered with leather and fur furniture and oriental rugs of various sizes, between which gleamed thin slices of hardwood parquet floors. Vases, gold cigarette lighters, ashtrays and small statues were scattered about as if on display at an antique shop.

"Please make yourself at home," Mr. Faust repeated. "Go on, Frankie, look around all you want. It will be a few minutes, I'm afraid, until our supper is delivered. Mr. Polite and I will just sit here and chat and you go on, make yourself at home. My home is your home, young sir." His big wide face cracked open into a watermelon smile and he bowed ceremonially, his belly contracting like a folded pillow. "Go on, don't be shy." He made a shooing motion with his hands, as if he were talking to a cat that had gotten on the sofa.

Frankie wandered around the big living-room, examining the photographs and paintings. The latter had that textured nubby feeling of oils but otherwise made no impression on him; the glassed photographs, though, were of people who looked familiar and he peered at them with curiosity while Mr. Faust and Mr. Polite conferred in whispers. Several of the photos were of actors he recognized, including one of Gary Cooper wearing shorts and a T-shirt and a baseball cap, a tennis racket under his arm, and looking impossibly young. There were two baseball players, a football player grinning toothily over massive shoulders, and a black prize fighter whose picture Frankie had seen before, on the sports pages of *The Daily Mirror*, his arms glistening with sweat, nostrils flared with menace. Over a long, chocolate brown leather sofa, there was a large framed colour photograph, the pink of flesh so bright it looked more like a painting, of the pope, his face almost gaunt, his arms spread wide, speaking to a crowd in an ornate, baroque square.

Frankie edged his way cautiously toward a corridor leading to the rear of the apartment. When he got there, he studied a painting closest to the doorway with great interest, observing Mr. Faust and Mr. Polite out of the corner of his eye. The two men were seated on a pink velvet love seat, their knees touching, heads close together, speaking seriously in whispered tones. Mr. Faust's back was to Frankie, and the fat man's bulk blocked him from Mr. Polite's view. He slipped quietly out of the room.

He went past a bathroom and a book-lined den to the door at the end of the hallway, beyond which was a bedroom with its own small bathroom and dressing area, a massive, canopied bed and French doors opening onto a balcony overlooking the grounds of the hotel. Frankie quickly retreated and went into the large marble bathroom, dominated by a built-in stepdown tub big enough for half a dozen people, and urinated as quietly as he could into a glistening blue bowl. It had been hours and he was bursting. The toilet flushed with a soft vacuum swish rather than a splashing and gurgling of water. He washed his hands in a marble basin cool and smooth as glass, the water hissing from a gleaming, arched faucet controlled by glass and gold handles. The smell of the bathroom was a combination of talcum powder and spices like those he had caught whiffs of in bakeries and in a woman's handbag he once stole, but knew no names for.

He was in the study, reading the titles of books, when he heard a soft chiming he knew must be the doorbell. A minute or two later, Mr. Faust called. Frankie had a leatherbound copy of *The Arabian Nights* with beautiful coloured illustrations in his hands and he quickly shoved it back on the shelf.

"Where's Mr. Polite?" he asked when he came back into the living-room. Mr. Faust was leaning over a cart like the one they had passed in the hallway, a silver tray cover in his hand and a pleased look on his face, but the white-haired man who had brought Frankie here was not in sight. For the first time since arriving at the hotel, he felt a twinge of panic, like a finger of chalk running up his spine.

"Our mutual friend has had to run off, I'm afraid," Mr. Faust said, shaking his head slightly, just enough to set his cheeks shaking. "It was quite unexpected, since I know he was looking forward to a small repast and an evening of conversational cheer with us. When our supper arrived, there was a note for Mr. Polite that had just arrived downstairs. Some urgent business, I imagine, or a family matter. Mr. Polite's mother lives not too far from here, and she is elderly and not all that well, poor dear. He didn't confide in me. He did assure me, however, and ask me to assure *you*, that he would return to collect you, my boy, and made me promise to look after you in his absence, as if such a promise were necessary." He snorted, making his nostrils flare like those of the prize fighter in the photo on the wall behind him. "It will be a pleasure. Now, come look at how much food there is for us. I had ordered for three."

Frankie was starving, so he came into the room, but slowly. Mr. Faust was taking the covers off the trays on the cart and he could see piles of neatly quartered sandwiches, bowls of pickles, potato salad, potato chips and pretzels, stacks of cheese and deviled eggs, a platter of pastries oozing red and yellow fillings, glistening with icing. There was an ice bucket filled with bottles of beer and pop, cold steam rising from the glass like a beckoning, ephemeral hand.

Mr. Faust observed him, his thick lips puckered into a rosebud. "You're not frightened of me, are you, Frankie?"

"No, sir."

"Ah, you say that with conviction, young sir, but something about your demeanor belies that, I'm afraid."

"Sir?"

Mr. Faust showed his marshmallow teeth. "I mean, you *look* like maybe you are."

74

"No, sir, I'm not afraid." To prove it, Frankie stepped up to the cart, smiled at Mr. Faust and let his eyes feast. His stomach was growling.

"Well, good. You're obviously a young man who knows his own mind and is not afraid to state his own case forcefully. I like that in a man, young or old. Keep true to that, Frankie—it will serve you in good stead in the world so loudly advertised as cold and cruel but most notable for its subtlety, its penchant for irony. Let's eat then. Here's plates. Help yourself, don't be bashful, I know you won't be. Everything has to be eaten or it will be thrown away, those are the rules in a hotel just like in a restaurant, wasteful but hygienic and hygiene must be served, god knows. Don't be polite—our friend *Mr.* Polite wouldn't be, of that you can be sure. That's right, have more of that. This salad is a specialty *de la maison*"—he beamed, his small green eyes shining—"that means it's our chef's special pride. Now, sit down here, beside me. Soda?"

The fat man kept chattering on while they ate but Frankie was too intent on the food to pay much attention. "Mr. Polite tells me you're off to see the world," he said.

Frankie nodded, his mouth full. "Montana," he mumbled.

"Ah, yes, the life of the cowboy. Very romantic. I know a few cowboys, real ones, I mean. Rodeo cowboys. They do the same sort of thing that men before them did every day to earn a living, and a mean living at that, but they've mastered the techniques and made them into a sport. Most fascinating to watch. Most fascinating men."

Crumbs cascaded from his mouth and clung to the nubby fabric of his suit jacket and tie. He excused himself and went into the bedroom to change, returning in a tent-like satiny smoking jacket and ascot, both the pale orange colour of salmon flesh Frankie had seen in the window of the fish store on 125th Street.

"Most commendable, taking off on one's own to see the world and make one's own way in it," Mr. Faust said, re-settling himself on the leather sofa, which let out a sigh beneath his weight. "You might not believe it, to see me now, but when I was your age, or perhaps just a little older,

I was a cabin boy on a merchant steamer, plying the North Atlantic."

Frankie looked up with interest and the fat man winked, the loose flap of his eyelid coming down like a window shade, then springing up.

"The things I could tell you about *that*. But it makes no difference how one goes about it, running off to the sea or to become a cowboy or to join a circus, for that matter, as a dear friend of mine did, the important thing is to *do* it. To run off."

He beamed, wiping the watermelon smile with a linen napkin. Mr. Faust's face was something like what Frankie would have expected Santa Claus to look like, with red cheeks that seemed to be puffed out, dark eyes made small by the rolls of flesh pocketing them in, a nose like a walnut, bloated and veined. His chins cascaded into themselves, like a Chinese box set. The mouth, pink and soft, was strangely small—much too small to have consumed all that must have been required to build the bulk of the body which depended on it.

Frankie ate and ate until he was stuffed, the variety and idea of the food pushing him on way past hunger. He was tired, and the exertion of all that eating now made his head begin to fill with cotton, his eyes to sag. He didn't know what time it was, but it had been dark for a while and, through the thin white curtains blowing airily over the bay window, the lights of what appeared to be a city spread out in the distance, blinking, the occasional burst of neon colour punctuating the generalized glow of streetlamps. He wondered idly where Mr. Polite had gone and when he would be back. His friend hadn't actually said so, but he had given the impression that he was travelling west, and that Frankie could go with him as far as he went. With the ignorance and confidence of a 10-year-old, though, he wasn't worried. The Cadillac man would either come back or he wouldn't. If he didn't, there'd be other rides. Frankie was too sleepy to think on the problem for long.

He stretched and yawned, juggling his shoulders into the firm leather cushion, and Mr. Faust, who had been watching him intently, put the watermelon to work.

"Ah, Frankie, have enough?"

He nodded, eyelids drooping. "Yes, sir. Thank you."

"Good, good." Mr. Faust selected a tray at random—it contained several quarters of sandwiches—and waved it at Frankie. "Sure now? Don't be polite. Your stomach will never thank you for a nicety of the intellect like that."

"I'm not, sir. I'm full, honest. Thank you."

"Good, good." Mr. Faust put the tray down and looked at his bloated hands, which had neat, smoothly filed nails, each one big as a quarter. For the first time since they'd begun to eat, he was silent. He took a long cigar from a glass-lined silver humidor and rolled it appraisingly in his fingers before putting it into his mouth and reaching for a silver lighter in the shape of a goose touching down on water. The cigar, unlike Mr. Faust, was long and slender. He licked the length of it, with a tongue pink as a cat's and surprisingly dainty, just before lighting it, and then it was sleek and dark, like the body of a cat in flight.

"Frankie." Mr. Faust said the name quietly, then repeated it with more precision, breaking down the parts, as if it were a foreign word he had just heard for the first time. "Frankie. It's a nice name, rich in meanings." He squinted through the cigar smoke, which smelled rich and exotic, not like the awful stogies Frankie's father used to smoke occasionally, when he was feeling chipper. "Many layers of meanings. Frank. Straightforward, no beating around the bush, uncompromising. Strong. But, at the same time, suggesting something of the French, something subtle and continental, full of flavour and history." He shrugged, rolling the cigar between pudgy fingers. "And Frankie, of course, Frankie, *Frankie*, the colour that name conjures up, the romance." He tilted his face up, eyes raking the ceiling, the pudding of flesh that was his neck pulsing. *"Frankie and Johnny were lovers,"* he crooned softly, *"lawdy, how they could love."*

Frankie closed his eyes and let his chin drop into the hollow between his collar bones. The fat man's voice was soft and filled with moonlight, filled with the light of the streetlamp which poured into the window of his bedroom at home, filled with the sounds of the street where he lived.

"My name is John, you know," Mr. Faust said suddenly.

Frankie opened his eyes. The fat man laughed in a way he knew was forced, without real mirth.

"Johnny. Lord, it's been years since anyone called me that. Frankie and Johnny, that's us." Mr. Faust lifted the great weight of his haunches, tilted his hips and let his body descend closer to Frankie on the flattened leather cushions, which hissed beneath him. He put his hand on Frankie's leg, patting it, then squeezing the knee. "Yes, yes, Frankie and Johnny." He laughed again, this time with more conviction.

"Frankie. Is it Frank? Or Franklin? After our great, much mourned president? Or short for Francis? The great saint who the birds took for their own? Or what?" A cloud of bluish smoke hung around his head like a swarm of tiny flies, but behind the pockets of flesh his eyes swam like green moons in a buttery sea.

"Francisco," Frankie said with distaste, grudgingly. "But I don't like that. Everybody calls me Frankie, even my father."

"Ah, Francisco. Now *there's* a name with magic in it. Magic and romance. Spanish, you know, is the loving tongue."

He pronounced the last two words with a reverence that made Frankie look at him more closely. Spanish was a language that he knew, but he was sure he had never heard that expression before. It made him think of his mother, who had died the day he was born. Spanish had been *her* language.

"It's okay," he said, perhaps to hide his shame.

"Okay?" Mr. Faust smiled. "I understand. It sounds... *foreign*, doesn't it? Someday, I assure you, you'll appreciate it. Take my word for it, young sir. And your father, is he a poet? An admirer of Garcia Lorca, no doubt. Only a poet would bestow on his child a name with such poetry in it, such *fragrance*."

Frankie giggled. "He's a mailman. He plays the trumpet

78

and he likes to think he's a jazz musician, but he's only a mailman, he delivers the mail, that's all." He said that in a burst, with such bitterness he surprised myself.

Mr. Faust observed him thoughtfully. "Ah, a mailman and a musician." He peered at Frankie, puffing on his cigar, while he rolled those words around in his mind. "A *messenger* and a musician. Then I was right. He *is* a poet. But not one who meets with your whole-hearted approval, that is plain to see for anyone who has eyes. Is he aware of your disapproval?"

It seemed like such a silly question that Frankie couldn't think of anything to say in response. He shrugged. Mr. Faust studied him, then sprang to his feet with a surprising agility.

"Well, no matter, none of my business, anyway, is it? And it's getting late, there can be no denying that. We should be thinking about getting off to bed. You've had a long day, so Mr. Polite tells me, and you must be tired. No, I can *see* you are. And here I am, babbling on, keeping you up when there's nothing you'd like better than to slip into dreamland, am I not correct?"

Frankie stretched his arms but wouldn't let himself yawn. "No, that's okay. I'm not so tired."

The split watermelon flashed in Mr. Faust's face. His belly jiggled right through the tent of his smoking jacket. "Good, good, that's what I like to hear. Never give in to the weaknesses and demands of the flesh. Very commendable. Still, the flesh must be served. The mind is king, but the body is the palace in which the king lives, and it must be maintained, so that the king should not be seen to be in even the smallest way shabby. Isn't that correct, Francisco?" He grinned, the grin turning quickly into an expression that was almost sly. "Now, what do you say to a bath? Something to spiff up the old palace with, one might say. A nice, warm sudsy bath to relax us, then it's off to bed. Did you see the, *ahem*, swimming-pool in the bathroom? It's a delight, let me assure you."

Ordinarily, the idea of a bath wouldn't have appealed to Frankie and he would have protested, but that gigantic marble tub conjured up such an exotic world of decadence and sweetness he couldn't resist. He had decided, much earlier in the day, to go where the adventure took him. "Okay," he said, and he let Mr. Faust lead the way down the corridor.

One whole wall of the bathroom, behind the massive tub, was glassed, and it joined a hinged skylight directly above. They stood for a moment in the doorway of the dark room, staring out at the night, stars twinkling above them, sparse city lights below. "Isn't that a lovely sight?" Mr. Faust said simply.

He turned on a dim, blue light and set water flowing in the tub. It gushed out of a dozen spouts set in the marble sides and in a thin, delicate stream from the penis of a bronze angel the size of a cat standing on a pedestal in the very centre of the tub. "My, my, but this cost a terrible fortune, but it's worth every penny," Mr. Faust said. "Every penny, every day."

"It's swell," Frankie said. His eyes were open wide and he couldn't take them off that bronze penis, that delicate arch of bathwater.

"Well, shall we?" Mr. Faust unbuttoned his smoking jacket and took it off, fastidiously hanging it on one of a dozen hooks beside the door. Beneath it, he wore a sleeveless undershirt and his arms were pale, hairless, sagging.

"You're going to take a bath, too?" Frankie asked. The notion didn't so much surprise as amuse him. The tub was certainly big enough for both of them, but he had never heard of such a thing. Shame filtered through him for a moment and he hugged his arms, as if he had a chill. He had a dim memory, suddenly sharpening into focus, of standing with his father in a public changing-room at Coney Island, each locker attended by a naked man and boy like strangely defrocked priests and altar boys performing some obscene ritual of a dark religion. He had been sickened—actually nauseated—by that endless row of flashing buttocks, the men's hairy and wrinkled, the boys' smooth and lean, like the flanks of cattle in a barn, the penises and scrotums hanging like vines and clusters of grapes from

80

each body, waiting for some vile hand to pick them. He hadn't wanted to take off his clothes, to expose himself, to become part of that vulnerability, but his father was already out of his shirt and pants, oblivious, his socks drooping, his shorts baggy and torn in spots, hair curling out from under his arms like licks of flame. "G'won, take off your stuff," he'd snarled, the words cracking down at Frankie like a slap on the ears. He had closed his eyes and fumbled for his buttons, taking off everything in a burst of speed, the way you jump into cold water to get it over with quickly.

He remembered all that while Mr. Faust was taking off his silk ascot and struggling the undershirt over his head.

"Don't you think the tub is big enough for the two of us?" the fat man laughed. "Damn this thing, why does it always have to catch on my elbows. There." He gave Frankie a sharp glance, saw his hesitancy and discreetly turned his back. "Go on, get undressed, Frankie," he said in a surprisingly gentle tone. "Don't be shy. We're men of the world, you and I, don't forget. We're runaways, men who run off to see the world, men who aren't afraid of life, who seize it and drink it up, down to the very bottom of the cup, then demand that the cup be filled again, right to the brim. Now…last one in is a rotten egg." Mr. Faust giggled and began to huff and puff his pants off.

Another memory broke the surface of Frankie's mind, like a fish in a lake breaching the calm of the water with a roll of flashing side to catch a fly. After the swimming that day, splashing through the waves in their trunks, he and his father had gone back to the locker-room and taken them off, then sat naked and streaming sweat in the Turkish bath at the rear of the bath house, men and boys with their heads lowered like supplicants in a *shul*, hair plastered to their bodies in thin, dark rivulets, sharing their vulnerability, drawing strength together from it.

He took his clothes off and lay them in a neat pile on a glass magazine table. The underwear was dirty and he stuffed it into one of the legs of his jeans, where it wouldn't be seen. He extended a toe into the frothing water that had filled a third of the tub by now. It was warm and sleek with soap and oil. "I just remembered something," he said, trying not too look at the huge pendulous moons of Mr. Faust's ass. "I thought I never took a bath with anyone else, but I just remembered I did, a Turkish bath. Does that count?"

Mr. Faust turned around and beamed at him, the watermelon splitting across his face. He was incredibly fat, with a roll of flesh like an inner tube around his middle. He wasn't circumcised, and his penis was like a thick sausage or a hank of rope hanging from the untidy package of his belly. There were hairs scattered across his chest and belly like weeds in a lawn and he was pale as the underside of a fish. Without knowing why, Frankie was washed over with a vague feeling of sadness for the fat man, as if he had just heard of a death in his family or some other great loss.

"Does that count? Why, it certainly does. A Turkish bath is one of the most delicious inventions of mankind, and it certainly is a bath. But"—he stepped toward the tub and put the toes of one swollen foot into the water—"there isn't anything as delicious as this, not in heaven *or* on earth."

There were steps going down into the tub and Mr. Faust negotiated them gingerly, then settled like a great walrus into the suds. He sat crosslegged, like a Buddha, the water lapping at his knees. "Come on in, Francisco. Tell me about this Turkish bath of yours. *This* city isn't sophisticated enough to have one, but I've been in many of them in my time. Tell me about yours."

"Look out," Frankie yelled, holding his nose and jumping into the water, sending balls of suds flying into the warm air above the tub. The water was actually deep enough for him to swim in and he splashed around for a moment, then claimed a spot across the tub from where Mr. Faust lay, grinning. He propped his neck against the rim of the tub, the water all the way up his skinny chest, slippery and warm, thick with bubbles that hid most of his lower body and made him feel at ease. He had a sudden image of himself curled up like a baby under his desk at school during an air raid drill. Miss Murphy, his teacher that year,

82

said the children should have clean, pure, gentle thoughts so if the bomb really fell they'd wind up in heaven. Tiredness wound its way through him like a lazy cat stretching in the sun, and he felt, inexplicably, *natural*, and content, as if he'd been travelling for a long time but had finally come home.

He told Mr. Faust about the Turkish bath, and about changing to their trunks in the locker-room—telling him details of feeling that he could never have told his father, but somehow had no hesitancy in pouring out now, to this stranger—and the fat man listened intently, with the kind of narrow-eyed interest adults don't usually waste on children.

"Thank you for sharing that with me," he said when Frankie finished. "I think I understand. I *know* I do. A similar thing happened to me."

"Oh, yeah?" Frankie said, only mildly interested, he was so sleepy. "To you?"

Mr. Faust nodded solemnly, looking slightly comical, since a puff of suds was on his nose. "My father was a physician, in a very prosperous community in Indiana. Do you know where that is, Frankie? A few states to the west —you'll pass through it if you continue your travels in that direction. He was an educated man, a refined man from whom, I'm happy to say, I acquired many of my tastes, but he was, ah, shall we say, just a touch arrogant? Pompous? Do you understand those words, Frankie?"

"Arrogant, I think. Not the other."

"Pompous. It means sort of what it sounds like: pomp, pompon. Puffed up." Mr. Faust laughed. "Not like me, I mean puffed up inside, thinking that you're very important. Have you heard the expression 'stuffed shirt'? That's what it is to be pompous."

"Oh, yeah." Frankie let himself slide deeper into the soothing water, right up to the crown of his head.

"Of course, my father was important, and he knew it. He was an extremely capable physician, and by far the most experienced one in our community. And he had business interests as well that made him quite influential. People sought out his advice, not only on medical matters, but on affairs of business, and even of the heart." Mr. Faust winked, a big, thick eyelid drooping down over one startlingly jade-green eye, then springing back up like a window shade with a tight spring.

"So he was important, but there is *so* much difference, isn't there, Francisco, between being important and *thinking* you are, even if, in fact, you are—if you see what I mean."

"I think so," Frankie said, although he didn't really. The warmth of the water was conspiring with his tiredness and the food to make him sleepier than he could ever remember being.

"Well," Mr. Faust said, waving his hand and stirring the suds, "pompous, he was that, surely, Father. But the point is, the reason I'm telling you this, Francisco, is that because he was so pompous, so arrogant, he was also intolerant of weakness, in himself, to be sure, but in others as well, including, all too often, his patients. Not a particularly sympathetic bedside manner, no, no, that was certainly not Father's way. Gruff, strict, demanding. But effective. He refused to let people lie back and feel sorry for themselves, refused to let them give up. None of my father's patients was ever sick a day longer than they *had* to be. None of them ever died unless the good lord absolutely insisted. Yes, effective, to be sure, but not very tolerant. No, no, not Father."

Mr. Faust's voice trailed off, and the sudden silence in the bathroom startled Frankie awake. When he looked up, he found the fat man staring at him as if surprised to have found a stranger in his tub. But, after a moment, Frankie realized he wasn't really looking at him at all—the puckered green eyes were unfocused, directed ahead but not seeing anything. Frankie made a little splash and Mr. Faust shook his head, like someone coming out of a doze in the back seat of an automobile.

"What was I saying, Francisco?"

"About your father...."

"Ah, yes. I started to tell you about being ashamed of being naked. I was. *Me*. Can you believe it? A fine figure of

84

a man such as myself?" The folds of flesh on his face and chest shook as he laughed. "Of course, when I was your age, I was more of a slim little charmer like you, and had no good reason to be ashamed to be naked. I don't know if I'd always been so, but all of a sudden I was. And it happened that the time came for our annual checkups, which Father performed himself on his children, boys and girls alike— yes, I have three wonderful sisters as well as two loyal and brilliant brothers—and it was my turn. *Take off your clothes*, Father said"—and here, Mr. Faust made his voice go low and gruff when imitating his father, then spring back to his natural tones, like a ball being forced beneath the water, then quickly rising to the surface—"but I felt I could not. *Take off your clothes, I said*, Father repeated, and I said to him, 'Father, I am not being willfully disobedient, but I feel I cannot.' *You cannot?* he exclaimed. *And why is that?* And, listen to this, Francisco, you may find this hard to be-lieve. I started to tell him. I said, 'Father, I'm ashamed to be naked in front of you.' And, instead of dropping to his knees and enfolding me in his arms, murmuring to me, reassuring me, explaining to me how silly I was being, how natural it is to be naked—in short, acting like a civilized man, acting the way you would expect a father to act to-ward his beloved young son—now, wouldn't you, Fran-cisco?—instead of doing any of that, listen carefully to this, Frankie—he slapped me."

Mr. Faust brought his open palm down hard on the sur-face of the bathwater, producing a sharp cracking sound that startled Frankie.

"Slapped me," Mr. Faust repeated, as if his face still tin-gled from that sudden blow. "Me, his son, his beloved son, eight years old. How old are you, Frankie?"

"Eleven. Almost eleven."

"Ah, yes, eleven. A good age to be, young sir. I was eight." He blinked, his face blank. "And then, then—listen to this very carefully, Francisco—then my father tore my clothes off me. I don't mean undressed me, I don't mean helped me off with my clothes, I don't mean unbuttoned my shirt—I mean he ripped my clothes off my back, literally, buttons and strips of cloth flying around his examining-room like feathers in a chickenhouse when the fox has gotten in. I mean tore off my clothes, every last shred, until I was standing naked in front of him, and then he said to me, *Ashamed to be naked, are you? Don't you ever say that to me again. And don't you ever be ashamed. Not of your body, or anything else that's part of you. Not ever.*

"And, do you know what, Frankie?" A smile suddenly spread across Mr. Faust's watermelon face.

"What?"

"I didn't cry. I imagine that surprises you, doesn't it? I wanted to cry, so badly, I think maybe you can imagine how badly I wanted to cry. Can you?"

"I guess so."

"Yes, I'm sure you can. I wanted to cry, but I didn't. I wouldn't let myself. I wouldn't give him that satisfaction. *Eight*, that's what I was, but I wouldn't give him that satisfaction. I just stood there, naked as the day I was born, and I held my shoulders straight and my head high, the way they taught us to at school and I'm afraid they don't anymore, and I didn't cry. And after a while my father examined me—took my pulse and blood pressure, listened to my chest and tapped on my back, peered into my mouth and ears and eyes, pressed his finger beneath my scrotum and told me to cough—and when he was through he said to me, *You're all right, boy, now put your clothes back on.* And I said, 'I don't think my clothes are suitable for wearing anymore, sir,' and he went to a closet and brought me a dressing-gown, the sort of thing he would give a woman patient to wear in the examining-room, and said, *Here, wear this up to your room and get dressed.* And I said, 'That's all right, Father, I can walk naked through the house, because I'm not ashamed.' And he looked at me so hard it was like one of his scalpels going through me, and I thought he was going to slap me again, but he didn't. All he did was hand me the gown and say, *Put this on, son,* in a voice more tender than I could ever remember hearing him speak."

Mr. Faust took a purple washcloth from a hook and lathered it with a bar of scented soap. "And you know something else, Francisco?"

"What's that, Mr. Faust?"

"I never was ashamed again. Of my body, I mean. To be naked." He laughed, making his cheeks jiggle. "Of course, there have been *some* things in my life I've been ashamed of. Not many, mind you—I've always tried to be a dutiful son—but some. And, please, Frankie, not *Mr. Faust*. Call me John, won't you? Or Johnny, better yet. Frankie and Johnny?"

Frankie nodded his head and they were silent for a minute. Finally, he said: "He never hit me."

Mr. Faust smiled. "Your father? He never slaps you?"

"No. Never. I don't think so."

"But he yells at you, I suppose. You said that's what he did in the locker-room."

"It wasn't really a yell," Frankie said. "That isn't what he does. Mostly, he don't say nothing. Just nothing."

Mr. Faust considered this, and his smile softened, his thick lips almost straightening. "All in all, Francisco, I'm afraid I'd have to say that was worse, far worse. At least when people yell they're talking to each other. When they hit each other, awful as that is, at least they touch."

He reached out to touch Frankie, but the tub was so large, they were so far apart, that he could only reach his foot. He patted it, and, in the slippery water, it felt as if a fish were brushing against Frankie, nibbling at his toes.

After a while, Mr. Faust withdrew his hand and rested it in his lap, with the other. He was watching Frankie, smiling, but he didn't say anything for a long time and his breathing grew heavier. Frankie thought he knew what the fat man was doing, although he hadn't ever done it himself. He'd heard other kids talking.

"Are you going to do something funny?" he asked.

Mr. Faust chuckled. "I'm doing something very funny indeed, but to myself, not to you. And you don't have to watch, if you'd rather not. Don't go away, please, but you can turn your head, or close your eyes, better. That's it, Francisco, why don't you close your eyes and just drift off to sleep."

"No, that's okay."

He didn't begin again right away, and when he did, it was a while before Frankie realized it. He was quiet, barely moving, his eyes never leaving Frankie, and the suds were thick around him. It seemed to take a long time.

"You can do it, too," Mr. Faust said, "if you'd like to. I can see you're old enough. I could help you, or you could do it by yourself."

"No, that's okay," Frankie said. He would have liked to try, but he didn't want to, either. He watched for a while, but then he made a boat with his hand and turned his attention to it as it skimmed through the water, like a sailboat on a windy sea. In a moment, he fell asleep in the warm water.

He woke up in Mr. Faust's arms, a towel big enough for the fat man wrapped around him. Mr. Faust was wearing a purple robe with satin lapels, and Frankie's cheek was pressed against the satin. The fat man lay him down on sheets that seemed just as smooth and cool and Frankie realized he was in the den, in a bed made from the sofa he had sat on earlier, reading *The Arabian Nights*.

"I'll just tuck you in and you can drift off back to sleep, Francisco," Mr. Faust whispered. "I'm afraid I don't have any pajamas your size, but would you like to sleep in one of my pajama tops?"

"Okay." He rubbed his eyes, sitting up, and put on the massive shirt. It was like a tent, but it was soft and he lay back again, snuggling into it like it was a cocoon that could keep him safe from everything, even being far from home, on his own, with a long way to go till Montana.

"You made me very happy tonight," Mr. Faust said from the doorway, just before he snapped off the final light. "Thank you."

"I didn't do anything," Frankie said, making a small shrug with his shoulders. "You don't have to thank me."

Mr. Faust smiled, his teeth a wide row of white seeds in the watermelon. "Do you have to *do* something to make someone happy? Can't you just *be*?"

Frankie was going to say something, but he was asleep

before he could.

In the morning, he was awakened by Mr. Polite, tugging the covers and poking his knee. "I brought you a present," he said, holding up a toothbrush. "The one you left in the car hardly had any bristles left on it. Your teeth will rot and fall out if you keep on brushing them with that dirty old thing, and you'll be a toothless old man before your time. Like me." He flashed a smile that showed lots of gum, but he seemed to have all his teeth.

"Come on, young man, we have to be on the road. The great vistas of the west call to us and time and tide wait for no man, or boy, either, I might add. By the time you're finished in the bathroom, breakfast will be ready."

In the bathroom, where Frankie broke in the toothbrush, he found his clothes neatly folded on a table, the underwear and socks and polo shirt washed and still warm from the dryer, which was good, since he'd drenched them with sweat the day before. There was a bowl of cereal, another of fresh strawberries and a pitcher of milk on a tray in the kitchen. While he was eating the cereal, the doorbell chimed and Mr. Polite went to the door, coming back with another tray, this one containing two dishes of scrambled eggs and bacon, a stack of toast and a pot of coffee for him, more milk for Frankie.

Mr. Faust was not in the apartment. "Oh, he's busy in the mornings," Mr. Polite said with a wave of his hand. He wore the same tweed jacket and blue slacks as the day before but his shirt seemed fresh. "You wouldn't believe the work involved in running a place like this. Now hurry up and eat. The sun is climbing in the sky and it will be hot on the road today."

Mr. Polite advised Frankie to go to the toilet before they left, so they wouldn't have to stop soon. "We're anxious to be on our way west, eh, Frankie?" He sipped delicately at his coffee cup, the rim barely making an impression on his wafer-thin lips, his fox-like eyes darting over the rim of his newspaper. "And don't forget your new toothbrush."

They went down the private elevator to the floor below,

where Mr. Polite steered Frankie wordlessly to the stairwell at the other end of the corridor. They walked down two flights to the fifth floor, then rang for the elevator. The young black man operating it looked Frankie over, then Mr. Polite, then looked away.

When the elevator doors opened, Mr. Polite took Frankie by the hand and they hurried through the lobby. There was no sign of Mr. Faust or the skinny desk clerk with the Adam's apple, or the woman in the long dress. Outside, the sun was dazzling, and Mr. Polite had been right, it was going to be a hot day. He gave his car keys to a shiny-faced kid decked out like the Philip Morris bellboy, and the kid, who looked barely 16, tipped his red hat and said, "Yes, *sir*, right away, sir," and ran down the steps like he was on the way to a ball game.

A woman with two small dogs on a leash walked by, looking at them curiously. Then Mr. Polite's powder blue Cadillac rolled up and they walked down the steps. Mr. Polite gave the kid a tip. "Thank *you*, sir, thank *you*," the kid said. They got in the car and Frankie was glad to see his crumpled paper bag on the front seat. Sure enough, though, the toothbrush was gone.

Mr. Polite turned on the air-conditioning and a cool hand closed over them like a breath. He drove down the long crushed stone driveway and through what appeared to be grilled gates without saying a word. Then they were on city streets and, abruptly, after a sharp turn, on a highway.

"Where is this place?" Frankie asked.

"You should be thinking about where you're going, Frankie," Mr. Polite said, "not where you've been."

They drove in silence. The sun was halfway up to the centre of the sky, and it was ahead of them, a little to the left. Mr. Polite wore his sunglasses, and Frankie turned the visor down and squinted.

"Aren't we going the wrong way?"

"It's just the way the road goes, Frankie. It loops back on itself, like life. Sometimes you think you're going one way but really you're going another way."

They passed a bunch of signs for Philadelphia and then

came to a big bridge over the Delaware and they were in New Jersey. "Just don't say anything, Frankie," Mr. Polite said. "Everything will be clear shortly. Did you have a good time last night?"

"It was okay."

He laughed and put a filter-tipped cigarette between his thin lips. "Did you get hurt at all?"

"Who, me? No."

"So you haven't lost anything but one day of your precious time, am I right?"

Frankie didn't know what to say to that.

"And you've got your whole life ahead of you, don't you?"

Mr. Polite turned the Cadillac off the highway at Cherry Hill and stopped at a gas station. "We won't be able to stop for quite a long while after this, so why don't you go to the toilet?"

"I went already. At the hotel."

"We're on our way west, Frankie, and it's a long way to go. Better to be cautious at the beginning of a journey than desperate at its end, I always say."

There was a blast of heat like an oven door opening when Frankie got out of the car. He was pretty sure what was going to happen. "Should I take my stuff?"

"Don't be silly, dear boy. I'll be right here when you get back. I'm just going to fill up."

But the Cadillac was gone when he came out of the men's room, and his paper bag was on the pavement where it had been parked. He checked to make sure the new toothbrush was there, and it was, along with all his other junk.

He asked the kid who was selling gas the way to the highway going west, and started walking, with his thumb out. He got a ride pretty quick, but it was going the wrong way and it took him a while to figure that out. Then some kids in an old Chevy jalopy picked him up but they were just tooling around, so he didn't get anywhere. In late afternoon, he was still near Cherry Hill and his brains were frying from the heat. He got off the road at a bridge and followed a brook through some woods till he came to a place that looked safe enough, and went to sleep on moss, up against a dead, fallen tree, his bag for a pillow. Later, he walked along a railroad track till he came to an old shack where someone, hoboes, he guessed, had made a fire and left it still smouldering. He found some crumpled up paper and the stub of a pencil and, using the back of a rusted out old wheelbarrow as a table, he started to write a letter to his father. As he'd done once before, he wanted to say he was sorry for running away, sorry he was always such a nuisance, sorry his father had to work those extra hours at Christmas, sorry about the lies he'd had to tell to keep his job.

He spent the night there, in the shack, hungry and shivering in the surprising chill, dreaming of the dinner cart in Mr. Faust's room. Next morning, he found his way back to the road and was just walking along, not even trying to hitch, when he saw the policeman coming. He thought to jump into the grass along the road, but it wasn't very high, and he didn't really want to.

Later, he remembered, his father had made a big deal out of his having been picked up there, in Cherry Hill. "Gone three days and you couldn't even get past New Jersey." His father said that often, hundreds of times, it seemed to Frankie, and he had burned to tell him that he had, but he couldn't, somehow, and he didn't. It wasn't merely that he sensed he had participated in something wrong—and he *did* feel some shame, though he remembered the advice Mr. Faust's father had given *him*—and there might be trouble if his father found out about it. For a brief moment, less than a day, he had slipped out of their world, his father's and his, not just its geography but its environment and its influence, and into another one, a world he hadn't even dreamed existed. For as long as he could keep it fresh in his memory, it would remain *his* world, completely apart from his father, and he wanted that, enough so that he was willing to bear the taunts.

"Here's the great adventurer, the Basque sheepherder, runs away from home for three days and can't even get past

92

New Jersey." Frankie could remember his father telling people that, poking him and chuckling, and even now the tips of his ears tingled with the memory flesh and blood carry of humiliation, long after heart and mind forgive.

"So I want you to know, finally, after all these years, that you were wrong," Frankie typed, "that I did go farther, not just past something as arbitrary as a river forming a state line, but past the kind of borders that men make for themselves, the kind of borders we create to define ourselves. I did go farther, and I guess I never stopped, even though I came home that time, and other times—maybe once you start, you never do stop till you get to where you're going."

It had taken him a long time to get here, to Montana, wherever or whatever that place is, but he *was* here, and he kept moving closer to something else he just remembered—just that moment—something that his father, in his spiritual moments, used to call the *source*, the place we all come from and, some of us, if we're lucky, go back to.

"I did get farther," Frankie wrote, although he was pretty sure he wouldn't mail this letter either. *"I did.* I just wanted you to know that."

Missing Notes

David Helwig

I

Hugo heard a voice speaking to him, would have said that although he could make out no words. It was like the insistent noises at night in the empty house. Hugo didn't believe in ghosts of course—he sees a dim figure reflected in the old TV set as he crosses the room, and that's ghost enough for him—and yet when he heard the voice, he would not have said it was imagined.

At the time this took place, he was alone in a church. It was one of those white wooden Prince Edward Island churches, old fashioned carpentry still plumb and level, well kept up and freshly painted, and when he tried the door, it was open, and he walked in. It was the graveyard he'd come to see. He was not, in the usual way of things, interested in genealogy. It had always appeared to him a sad pastime, a hopeless primitive attempt to find a place in the cold universe, but he remembered his Aunt Claire telling him how many of their ancestors were buried in this field, and it was just along the road, and when he arrived here in the cold early spring and carried his bag into Claire's house, he found that he wished, in his solitude and confusion, to make a gesture of filial piety He walked past the flat white stones set upright in the green grass, perfectly tended, the grass luminous with spring. He didn't care which were the ancestors, only to walk the earth over their bones. Rose was here somewhere. Was that the reason he'd come ? He looked past the bare branches of a birch tree, the buds swollen but not yet open, to the frame church, the white walls caught in momentary pale sunlight shining against a background of rolling grey clouds, and he was drawn to it. He didn't expect the door to be open. The light shone down on the plain walls, the waxed wood of the floor and the pews, the pulpit from which some early Scots preacher had made the fierce assertion of John Calvin's creed. In the shed behind the house, he had found a framed motto, handwritten in ornate letters. "Flee from the wrath to come," it said, and below that, "How shall we escape if we neglect so great salvation." He stood still, and the silence sang in his ears until he heard whatever voice it was and looked around him, and there was nothing but the light and the flow of time.

As he walked back down the road to the house, he reflected on the nature of ghosts. The voices of other times, the past, the future, the voice of desire, plain and hidden, the fears which were desire in dark clothing.

2

When he found the small figure in a box in a closet, the figure of a naked woman in dark brown wax, he knew who it must be. The long neck and rather wide flat breasts, the wide hips, it was his cousin Rose. Years before, Rose had gone away to study art. In Boston. Though all that was forgotten when she came back from away, found a government job and settled down to ten years of responsible work. He held the small naked figure, perhaps two feet tall, in his hands and thought that it must be something that Rose herself had made, probably in art school. Had stood in front of a mirror and her fingers had shaped this portrait of her young body. The figure was crudely enough done; Rose had not been greatly talented. He remembered the handmade Christmas cards she would send. The last time he recalled seeing her—on a short visit with his mother, who was recovering from some disaster and wanting the reassurance of her old home—he was nineteen, and they had talked mostly about the early summers they had spent together here.

He looked at the naked figure and tried to remember if he and Rose had once undressed for each other in one of the small back rooms of the house. He thought so. It was perhaps at the end of the summer, when he was about to leave, and they both understood that he might not come back. Two small white bodies shivering and staring at each other with the same blank awareness. Adam and Eve knowing everything, nothing. He left the nude figure in the closet. Already he was too aware that this should have been Rose's house, that it had only been left to him because of her untoward death in that car accident five years before.

It was only later that she began to come to him in the night.

3

After his wife left, Hugo had quit his job as a music teacher in a good private school, left behind the house on Long Island and moved into the city, where he found an apartment in the Village, small and too expensive, but he needed the noise of the city, the traffic, the danger. The living world, city streets, cars and crowds, they made him real. He watched from his window as his neighbours passed by. The print seller going to his small shop. A man with AIDS being walked to the corner by his friend. Hugo would go out in the streets and watch the unemployed young black men playing a fast pickup game of basketball at a small court on a corner at Seventh Avenue. Himself, he could make a living of sorts editing and proof-reading musical texts. When he was in university—in Toronto that was, another stage of his wanderings—he had supported himself as a copyist. He was careful and had a good hand. Now it was done on computers. It was all but unknown for anyone to copy musical text by hand, but there was editorial work to be done, and he did it well.

Until A. announced that she was leaving, he would have said he was a happily married man. As evidence, not once in the fifteen years of teaching music to adolescent girls in a private school had he been indiscreet. A couple of times there had been pupils who were too intense, perhaps a little mad, who made gestures toward him, and each time, at the first hint, he went to the school's principal and explained the situation, made sure that she sent him a memo acknowledging the discussion and the fact that he had initiated it. He was not going to be destroyed by some hysterical girl. Early schooled in the consequences of heedlessness, he was a prudent man. He was proper and respectful, but of course he was not innocent. He had never once touched a student, had never spoken an indiscreet word, but he had looked at the girls who were coming to the peak of their physical beauty, had watched how they moved in the provokingly sexy school uniforms, the short skirts and long socks, long bare legs—Julie Christie in *Doctor Zhivago*—breathed their smell, caught the scent of a new soap or shampoo, had in fact spent all those years in the grip of a fervid erotic awareness. A hungry soul in a garden. His manner was formal, but he was sure that at some level the girls-becoming-women knew him for what he was. His classes were all the better for the soft buzz of desire in the air. A string didn't produce music until it was stretched to a very high tension. Janet Yetkind, the school's art teacher was, he suspected, much like him in this way, a lesbian who adored her disciples but kept a discreet distance. Neither of them ever had discipline problems. During his last week at the school, he had been tempted to go to Janet Yetkind and discuss the matter with her, for old times' sake, more or less, but he decided against it.

A. had brought all this up—speaking in her small, now hardened voice—when she announced she was leaving. She told him that he came home every night smelling of adolescent sex. Well, he might have said but didn't, she came home from the city smelling of ritual slaughter. That was how he thought of it, her work in the brokerage, as bloodshed. A.—well brought up in a decent family—loved danger.

The end was calm. Over the years, A. had borrowed money from him to invest along with her own savings, had even got him to borrow against his salary and pension for her, and she had made herself, if not rich, at least safe from immediate disaster, and she had paid back his loans with interest, given him the house and gone away. He was set to learn the rules of a new life. In the morning he lay in bed, cold and shaking, and he began to suffer from spells of dizziness, nausea. He avoided friends out of the fear of becoming dependent and tiresome, and he managed to silence himself each time he was on the point of telling his students what had happened to him. Every smile troubled him; the freshening girls were no longer mere leaves and flowers. His fingers had wishes, he would find himself beginning a class with tears in his eyes or sitting behind a desk to conceal a persistent erection. He knew that he couldn't go on like this for long, and so he resigned before he got into some pathetic mess.

4

How he came to spend those childhood summers on the island: his parents had been ahead of their time in their devotion to marital disaster. Back then people stayed married, but not Ralph and Lou. They met during the war. If he had used that phrase—during the war—to his students, they would have been puzzled, but when he was growing up in Canada, even though various wars were to continue, it was understood that there was one real war, in perhaps the way that as a child he'd believed there was one real Santa Claus, in spite of the variety of department stores, each with a jolly old man. During the one real war, Ralph, who was an American sailor, got himself to Halifax where Lou was training to be a nurse, and against all sense, they had got married, Lou pregnant with his older sister, Linda. This was only the first evidence of Ralph's fecklessness. When last heard of, Ralph had been moving to New Mexico with his third wife, and now he was missing, as they said in the one real war, and presumed dead. Hugo owed to this vanished father his early musical education (by the time he was born, his father was closing out a stint as a military bandsman), a very careful nature (who not to be like), and his absurd name. His father wanted to name him after Hoagy Carmichael, his mother didn't, and somehow they compromised on Hugo, which gave Hugo, in spite of his careful nature, a dim view of compromise.

He always tells stories about his childhood in this tone. It is safest to think of it as a kind of comedy, and perhaps true.

It was in periods of maximum disorder that Hugo got shipped to the Island to stay with his mother's sister Claire, and he and Rose, much of an age, had been the closest of friends.

5

He sat down at the piano and his fingers tried to play a Beethoven bagatelle, but there were keys that didn't sound, others out of tune, and the bass had a loose vibration, as if the hammers were at the wrong distance from the strings. There were spaces in the sound and extra rattles, but he played the piece through to the end, with a certain delight in its strangeness. The spaces where the notes were silent made room for other, unwritten notes.

He was a little out of practice—he kept an electronic keyboard in his apartment, but didn't often play it—and his fingers were cold. The old furnace used a lot of oil, and he kept the thermostat turned low. Claire had let things go in the last years, probably in a kind of despair after her daughter's death, though she had taken the trouble to correct her will, leaving him the house—the farmland had been sold off years before—while her small nest egg in Canada Savings Bonds went to the church. She had called him once to tell him what she'd done. He wondered if it was a reward for the fact that he had got here from New York, a long day's exhausting trip by car, to attend Rose's funeral. When he heard the news, he climbed in the car and began to drive. Claire had recognized him instantly when he walked into the church, and she had left a circle of cousins to come to him and take his arm and lead him to the front pew to sit with her.

When Hugo heard from the lawyer in Charlottetown, a letter to tell him that he had inherited the house, he thought that perhaps Claire expected him to move to the Island and live there, and he himself had given the idea some consideration. He was alone now, with nothing to keep him in New York, but the Island had never been his home, not really, and for all his delight in its beauty and the astonishing quiet, the way he could hear the sound of the slightest breeze, the soft piping of a chickadee somewhere far off, it wasn't a place to settle. Certainly not to settle alone.

He had a phone number in his wallet, one of his former students he'd met at a concert at Lincoln Centre. Valerie Quinn: a tall elegant girl who sang alto. When he thought about her, he pictured her in her school uniform, not in the slightly military black outfit she'd worn to the concert. Recently, he'd taken to looking at the personals ads in the *New York Review of Books*, and the absurdity of that made him feel that it was time he did something about himself. He would sit in Central Park, watching a trim ageing woman riding her rollerblades with narcissistic abandon, and he'd think that she must be one whose brief notice he'd looked at, now just as glad he hadn't answered. Did he have the courage to start over? Dating, all the embarrassment. It was a comic muddle, this business of arranging life. Better to be in the power of the ghosts.

6

He couldn't move, and he wasn't sure whether he was awake or asleep. Something in his throat was preventing him from breathing properly, and the temperature of his body altered from cold to hot every few seconds. There was someone in the house, and yet he could see only empty rooms and doorways. The figure of the wax sculpture drifted through the rooms, in a kind of invisibility that he ought to understand but could not. There was a weight on his body that was concentrated in the impediment to his breathing, and yet he felt that if she would come and lie with him, the weight would be eased. It would melt against him and he would be safe, but it didn't come any further than the edge of his vision. If he could call out her name, she might come to him, but he was too choked to speak.

The house was shaking in the wind, and there was no hope of safety. All he could do was wait, and there was a happy sense of inevitability, he was calm, and the noise of the wind stopped, and everything was perfectly still, while the figure of the naked woman stood in the empty room. Rose was watching him. There was something she had to tell him. Then he heard a voice without speech, and she was gone. The house made a soft groaning, then a clicking in the walls, then there was the creak of a floorboard. This was the natural world calling out for the return of all that had been.

7

He stood at the edge of the garden looking down at the first dark green of the strawberry plants appearing from under the fallen leaves. A cold breeze shook the trees, a wind coming off the water, still the feeling of winter. He had never known the Island in winter. Always summer and sun as the two children sat there between the rows and picked the red berries. When Rose found a very fat juicy berry she would give it to him and watch him crush it in his mouth, the acid sweetness of the juice touching his lips and making them darker red. He couldn't understand this, how she gave him the best ones. At home with his sister Linda, he had to fight for his share of everything, had to make deals to ensure some level of fairness. Linda was fierce and determined and full of anger and cunning, and it took all his cleverness not to be defeated and become her slave, while Rose always liked to see that he had the biggest serving, the sweetest berry.

The strawberry leaves grew in sets of three, like giant serrated clover, dark green against the rusty coloured earth between the rows, and he could feel the heat of the sun through the straw hat that Aunt Claire had given him to wear. He and Rose were putting the fruit in little wooden boxes, and when a box was full, one of them would take it in the house. When there were enough boxes, Aunt Claire would make jam. The air was full of the sweet smell of the hay that Uncle Evan was cutting in the next field. Rose was giving him another berry, but he shook his head. Her face, pink with the heat of the sun, was freckled over her nose, the eyes, blue of sky or of forget-me-nots, bright and intent, and puzzled.

"Don't you want it?" she said.

"We have to pick them."

"There's lots and lots."

She held the berry out to him again, and he took it, and her face watched with pleasure as he ate it. He lifted his head, and he could see the window of the little back room where he slept, the room next to Rose's, down the low hall under the sloping roof. When he wasn't there, the room was empty, waiting for him, the book he'd been reading spread out on the bed, or so he supposed, not being there to see. He felt someone watching him from that window. Tonight when he went to bed, he'd look out here and see the berry patch.

When they'd finished picking the berries, and maybe helping to make the jam, they were going to play their duet on the piano. He played better than Rose, but her parents said she had to practise anyway. Music was something Ralph did, and Hugo wasn't too impressed with anything Ralph did; if Hugo was clever at music, he might turn out to be like Ralph, who was no damn good. He turned and watched Rose's face under the straw hat, the way she picked the berries, carefully and with concentration, as if they could feel her fingers touching them and must not be frightened. Sometimes he would look, and find she was studying him, and then she would declare that she knew what he was thinking. He didn't dare challenge her to read his mind for fear that her claim might be true. Though he was almost sure that it wasn't. Almost.

Hugo stood alone in the yard, and the cold spring wind made him shiver as he wondered about the truthfulness of his memories. Did those things really happen? Something like that. Certainly all through the season, the two of them would be sent out to pick berries, and they would eat them for dinner and help Aunt Claire make them into jam. Later in the summer, they would drive to the blueberry barrens. It was part of the old life of seasonal necessities, a life that was gone now.

8

How he met A. and came to get married: Hugo was a music student at the University of Toronto, and A. was at Smith but came to Toronto on a one-year exchange, and they met through a woman friend of his, a church organist who was also a don in the residence. A. was small and had a little voice, a sexy whisper that reminded him of old Marilyn Monroe movies, and her American accent took him back to places he'd lived with Ralph and Lou when they were still together. At that stage Ralph was somewhere with a second wife, and Lou was living in Oshawa and working as a nurse in one of the car plants.

Hugo never had any doubt about who was in charge. A. was. She was a virgin when they met, but it was soon clear that she had selected him to be her first lover, perhaps only because he had a basement room with its own entrance, and that allowed a certain amount of privacy. Maybe it was because his father was an American. He never knew. What he knew was that virginal A. had put herself on the pill, and then put herself in his bed. Hugo had been planning to go down to the Island after his graduation, perhaps to look for work there, someplace safe and familiar, but he and A. couldn't keep their hands off each other, and before he knew it, he was checking on whether he could work in the States. Because his father was American, it was surprisingly easy.

Two years later, they were living in a small apartment on Long Island, and he was teaching while A. was a messenger for a brokerage house, a job she got because her father knew one of the partners.

Hugo can never find the appropriate tone for this story. He's never been quite sure whether it is a comedy and if so just what kind of comedy. Once A. left, he felt that he should be able to see it all in a new light.

9

No matter how he tried, he couldn't get warm. He had two sweaters on and a scarf around his neck. He didn't own long underwear. He stood by the back window of the room where he'd slept when he was a child here, and looked out over the long grass of what had once been a lawn, past the tangle of the overgrown garden, last year's plants with a hint of green here and there. The woods beyond were misted with a light rain. Some of the spruces were dying, the branches bare, covered with fungus of a beautiful grey green. It was a haunted, ruinous landscape now, until the leaves came. The leaves were usually out before he arrived on the Island for the summer, though he was once taken out of school before the end so that Ralph and Lou could set out on some hopeless adventure, as cook and bar manager for a resort in upper New York State, something that wouldn't work out and would give them subjects for argument for the next several months. Linda would be sent to Ralph's mother and Hugo to the Island to Evan and Claire.

His Uncle Evan was a silent man, probably not unkind, it was hard to tell. Hugo knew that Claire and Rose liked having him with them for the summer, and he always hoped that Evan didn't mind. If he'd been a son, rather than a nephew from away, Evan would have started to teach him farming, but as it was, he was left to the women. He read books and played the piano, and on Sunday they all went to church. Hugo listened to the organ and wondered what it would be like to play it, but he could never bring himself to ask Mrs MacDonald to let him try.

The raindrops were heavier now as they struck the glass of the window and hung there or slid down, and the woods were dim through the wet pane. In the ghostly grey light between the bare trees, he saw something move then disappear behind a tree. He leaned closer to the glass to try and see more clearly, then saw it again, for a moment, a woman, who stood and looked back toward the house, her eyes lifted to the window where he stood as if she could see him there. She was dressed in something dark, like an overcoat, and he couldn't make out her features, and then she walked away into the dead forest.

He was shivering as he waited to see if she would return, but there was no sign of her; there was nothing but the rain and the wet trees, so at last he turned away, went down the narrow back stairs to the kitchen and plugged in the electric kettle he'd bought and made some instant coffee. The fridge didn't seem to be working, so he was using a jar of whitener. With his hands clasped around the cup for warmth, he went into the front room and sat down at the piano. He let his hands settle on it, and he began to invent a little melody that avoided the missing notes, and as he played it through, it seemed to have words, the words of an old hymn he'd been taught in the Sunday school in that white church up the road. The odd tune shaped around the missing notes provoked equally odd harmonies, and when he had it worked out, he took a piece of paper and sketched a version of it so as not to forget. He'd never written music except arrangements for his students to play or sing. As he scribbled the last notes of a figured bass, he heard a knock at the front door. He set aside the piece of paper and went to answer it.

He didn't recognize the woman who stood there facing him. She was his age with thick blond hair and eyes of a very pure blue. There was something familiar about her face. She wore a dark overcoat, and he wondered if she could be the same woman he'd seen in the woods behind the house.

"There's something I have to tell you," she said. "It wasn't the way they said at all."

"I beg your pardon?"

"The way she died, it wasn't an accident."

"You mean Rose?"

"You can't believe what people will say. They never understand."

The wind was blowing the cold rain into his face.

"Would you like to come in?" he said.

"No," she said. "One thing leads to another. It's just that you're here, and someone should know."

"Are you talking about Rose? Is that it?"

"You can't believe everything you hear."

"She died in a car accident five years ago. I was here for the funeral."

"What's an accident?" she said, her eyes looking at him and then past him into the house, as if she expected someone to appear from behind him. "Who knows what was going on in her mind, what broken promises?"

"You know about that? She told you something?"

"I've said my piece," she said, turned and walked from the door out the road, turned left and began to walk through the rain, her head down, the water soaking into the cloth of the black overcoat. It was like a coat his mother wore when he was very young, the same colour and cut. There was no sign of any car that might have brought the woman here.

"Can I give you a ride?" he shouted after her, but she didn't look back. He closed the door and went back to the piano, glanced at the notes he had written, but they seemed to make no sense. He decided that he shouldn't leave the woman out there getting soaked, ran out to the rented car that was parked beside the house and drove down the road after her, but he couldn't find her.

When he got back to the house, he thought about Rose, the last disastrous seconds before the car hit a bridge abut-

ment, the woman's hints. Broken promises. Hugo didn't
make promises.

10

What Hugo sees when he wanders through the house,
looking at things: in the front room was an old stuffed
chair, upholstered in a dark red fabric that he remembered
from visiting the island as a child. The fabric was heavily
worn, the nap rubbed off in places, but the cloth has never
worn completely through. It was the chair where Evan
would sit after dinner and sometimes doze off for a few
minutes. Over the back of the chair was a crocheted cover
in an orange and black pattern, colours that clashed pain-
fully with the colour of the chair. Across the room was the
small black and white television set on a long coffee table
and beside it a lamp with a glass shade. On the side wall
was the old mahogany piano. Behind the front room, the
dining-room with its heavy oak table and chairs, too big for
the space, the glass fronted cupboard full of dishes against
the side wall.

   In the kitchen, there was a mark on the linoleum where
the old cookstove had sat, and a stovepipe hole in the
chimney behind, covered with a round tin cover held in
place by light metal springs. The replacement was an electric stove, with various marks and stains from Claire's later
days, when she wasn't in any state to keep things in order,
not strong enough. The old cupboards were painted in a
pale green that had faded toward grey. In places the wall-
paper had pulled away from the plaster, and in others it had
been glued back but with creases and wrinkles. There was a
brown water stain in the shape of a bird. A church calendar
hung on the wall near the back door, and on the wall a
print of Banff National Park, a lake of an unnatural blue
and snow-covered mountains.

   On the stairs, the rubber treads were ripped, and at the
top the hall was dark. The bulb in the overhead light had
burned out and Hugo hadn't changed it. The top of the

high veneered chest of drawers in Claire's room was crowded with family pictures. Hugo liked to study the one of Claire and his mother when they were girls, the two of them side by side in front of a farmhouse, an unknown man by the far corner of the house, staring with what might be curiosity or hostility.

The room that had been Rose's, back when they were children, was empty, except for a narrow bed and a small blue-painted chest of drawers with nothing in it. There were pictures of her in Claire's room, but here there was no trace.

Hugo had chosen to sleep in the back room where he always slept when he was sent here for the summer. There were clean sheets on the bed, as if it had been prepared for him, though there were also cardboard boxes filled with folded rags, old copies of Reader's Digest, odd dishes. Propped against the wall was the framed motto he had found in the shed. "Flee from the wrath to come. How shall we escape if we neglect so great salvation?" The words went round in his head and made as little sense as a nursery rhyme. When he stood at the window, he saw the garden and the woods beyond. Just outside the bedroom door was the narrow stairway that led down to the kitchen.

Hugo knew that to sell the house—and that was the only thing to do—he should empty it out and leave it clean and ready for someone to move in, but he couldn't bring himself to change anything. He camped out here, in the rain and fog of a maritime spring, as if he were waiting for something, perhaps for the leaves to come out, the wild cherry to blossom, the bed of strawberries to flower and bear fruit.

One evening, in a light rain, he walked up the church-yard again. He'd found an old slicker of Evan's in the shed, and he wore it, but the rain blew into his face. Still he kept walking, as if he might have an appointment there, as if the anonymous ancestors were waiting for him. When he arrived, he walked among the graves that rose from the wet grass, the old white stone pitted and pocked. He stopped in front of one of the higher stones and read the names. Four children of the family had died within a period of two years, between 1892 and 1894. Little figures lying in the dark, a mother or father watching by the yellowy light of an oil lamp. A child died, a child died, a child died, a child died. What had that woman said? Broken promises. Hugo had no children. Sometimes he thought his students were his substitute, a hundred daughters, he the lustful patriarch watching their growth into beauty. They were gone now. Everything from the past was gone, and as he looked across the grass that shone in the rainy light, he was one of the dead. He saw himself, standing here among the graves, as a ghost, a figure trapped between the world and memory, light shining through him, a quiet old man searching the past. Rose's grave was here, but he didn't look for it.

The rain was cold on his face and was soaking into his trousers. As he walked back to the house, he hummed the tune he'd made up, but he couldn't quite remember the words of the hymn that went with it.

11

She had come to him again. In the doorway, with the empty rooms beyond her, and with a promise of peace and calm. The body wavered between a dark figure of wax and a white figure of flesh, and he was confused about which one would come and lie with him, but he longed for her to come, and yet he was unable to move to go to her. He was paralyzed, and the figure did not come to him, yet he thought that she was speaking and that he could almost hear a strange babble of words, or perhaps not words, perhaps only the soft crooning of desire. Then he knew it was not that either, but that she was telling him secrets, offering him knowledge of death.

"Tell me again," he said, though the words were not spoken aloud.

"We are many," she said. "The wax is formed and melted and then remade."

He was at first moved by the words and then disappointed. A formula, motto from a homily.

She was lying on top of him, and her body was soft against his, sighing as she vanished, the wax soaking into his skin, as she became part of his body, and he was heavy and yet full of happiness, then he knew that she would never come back to him.

Hugo is awake, or believes he is, and remembering. The two children are on a beach. The sand of the beach is dark red and above, the cliffs are a flatter more intense shade of the same colour, and the grass has a tint that is luminous, blue-green, bright. The sun is shining down, and the two children play at the edge of the cold water, and if they look up, they can see across the choppy water to the horizon, where somewhere northeast across the Gulf, Newfoundland rises. Down past the beach, there is a small lighthouse, and a harbour with fishing boats. The two children are building forts or castles out of the sand, and they are dreaming of the future.

"I know what you're thinking," Rose says. "I can tell."

In the morning, he will drive to town and talk to a real estate agent, put the house on the market. There is nothing else to be done. There is nothing to be done with the past except to remember it; or to forget.

12

Hugo back home in New York: he stood by the window of his apartment and watched the man with AIDS being taken along the street by his friend. He moved very slowly now. Soon he was going to die, and his progress, step by step, was an act of fierce determination. His face was all bone, with a thin wrapping of skin. Coming the other way was a young black woman, short, with heavy breasts and hips, and it was as if she might have been deliberately set there as a contrast, an icon of the fullness of flesh.

When Hugo arrived, there were three messages on his answering machine, one from A. to call her if he wanted a good tip on the market, one from a music publisher offering him work, and one from Valerie Quinn, who said she had just heard somewhere that he was living alone—he hadn't explained anything when they met—and suggested they go out for dinner. A tall elegant girl who sang alto and would wish to make him happy. So there it was, three calls: offering him money, work and love.

The two gay men had reached the corner and were coming back. Another, older man had joined them, and Hugo thought that he knew him from somewhere.

13

His last day on the Island, he went back to the graveyard. The church, still dedicated to its imperative, now much-abandoned god, kept up by his loyal rearguard, a place to listen for some transcendent voice, a place of decency and vengefulness, shone white at the end of the lane, and he stopped to look toward it through the delicate half-open leaves that hung from the drooping branches of an old birch. In the morning he will leave, but this evening he has come along the road, his coat held tight around him to keep off the wind. The house was more than ever full of noises, voices of old wood crying out to him not to abandon them, but it has been put up for sale, and it will go to a stranger, and the old life will be taken from it and some new life will come.

In a week, if the weather is warm, all the leaves will be out. Already there is a dust of pale gold brushed over parts of the woodlands, but now he is in a hurry to be away. He will not wait for the beauty of the leaves. He has come here once to pay homage to the ancestors, and then he will abandon them.

Now he walks between the graves, his eyes catching a name, a date, aware of a hundred stories, untold and lost, and for a moment he has a certain sympathy for the genealogists and their brave, sturdy attempt to salvage a fact or two from the great silence, a chart that puts names in order, abstract and arithmetical, but an act of saving all the same.

A country graveyard reminded you of the old cycle of life, the rebirth of the natural world in the sap that plumped the buds, the grass that would be wild over all this if it hadn't been regularly trimmed. Yet it was trimmed, and the names were cut into each stone, the human record kept in order.

When he looked up, he saw there was another figure in the churchyard, close to the edge under the low branches of a large tree. The man was looking toward him, not so much toward as past him, as if he could see something beyond, and Hugo was convinced that the man could see Rose there, behind him, that she had returned to Hugo from another time, and that she was reading his thoughts. As he studied the man, who was partly hidden by the bare branches, Hugo heard a voice speaking to him, but the words were inapprehensible. All he can hear of the voice is the tone, the lost music.

There Are Bodies Out There

Leon Rooke

"Bud?"

"Yes."

"Where was I?"

"Jack Dreck."

"Jack?"

"Yes."

Okay. Jack Dreck, his black slick hair, his white bony hairless ankles, is reading the fine newsprint through splayed knees, going uh-oh, there's mayhem in Angola, uh-oh, them bikers over in Enfield are on the war path.

Like if he don't tell us the latest then we are never to know civilization's carrying on.

Ugg, I goes.

Outside the EatRite this is, on the loading ramp: me and these gooneybirds grabbing the break.

Mental don't want any, he goes. He's off carrots. He's into unwashed spinach, so's he can tongue the grit.

Ugg, I goes, pulling a face.

"Grit's good on yous," Mental goes. "Yous a kid, yous dint eat dirt?"

No, I dint, I goes.

"I dint either," goes Jack Dreck from Meats.

Dint is how them two speak. Juice them till doomsday, they don't never catch on. They's I.Q. below sea-level, see?

"Bud?"

"Yes?"

"See?"

"Yes. I see. Go on."

"Where was I?"

"Sea-level."

"Oh. Okay."

Okay. Then I'm going Ow! again. I'm scratching like fury at what is crawling up my leg. A huge bug invisible to the naked eye is creepy-crawling under my stretch tights, me with my whole hand under there zitching away. Bedbugs, could be, from the girl's scummy habitat.

The bug moving on, taking more snips. Me going Ow, Ow, Ow! digging the nails.

There's blood under the full five, though no bug.

I'm looking back at Jack Dreck gawking at me zitch. "Need help," he goes.

Flicking his tongue as he scans the works.

"Pubescent flesh," he goes. "Ain't it rich?"

Me and him and Mental all shaking into hysterics. Cackle, cackle, we goes.

My mini, good softest leather costing a pearl, is hiked up over my hips.

Jack Dreck, or Dread we call him to his rear-end, is rearranging his keg seat. He only sits his fat bum on a thing with newspaper rolled in a back pocket to keep dreaded diseases at bay. He won't sit in movie house or café without his newsprint. Trains, buses, forget it.

"Yous remind me the time I had the crabs," he's going now. "Yous scratching like that. Man, did them buggers itch me. Yous put them louse under me pap's jeweller piece yous could see theirs eyes. See these, like, cauliflower ears them crabs had. Their feet, their big teeth."

Double ugg, I goes. Don't say 'yous'.

Mental, he's swinging his head to and fro, like as how it's magic, lips to part and form words.

"I pass them crabs on to sixteen bedmates," Jack Dreck goes. "I couldn't accept the firm knowledge I had them crabs. See what I'm saying?"

Me and Mental going Uh-huh.

"Or I'd of went to a doctor."

"Un-huh," goes Mental. "Would of had."

Un-huh, un-hum, him going.

"My pistol leaky too. Yellow dribble night and day. My womenfolk thought it was I couldn't refrain from dwelling on them."

Ugg, I goes. That's horrific, Jack.

"I was young," he goes. "Crabs won't going to kill me."

"It won't going to kill him," goes Mental.

There's birds up in the sky, breaking fast as can shoot. The climate is turning goose-bumpy.

"But after a year," goes Jack Dreck—"after a year, year or two. After a duration, them crabs expire of old age. Jack is his noble pure self again."

That'll be the day, I goes, to Jack Dreck's grin.

Then he's got to show me and Mental how it was he went through them years, zitching night and day his beleaguered scrotum.

"Scrotum?" goes Mental.

Me and Jack Dreck dissolving into fits when Mental goes, "What's scrotum?"

"Yous family jewels," goes Jack Dreck. "Man, I was covered like plaster."

La, la, I goes, watching them birds.

Up in the brainless sky the clouds in a minute have turned cyclone grey. The cloudies are twisting theirselves inside out.

The wind going whoosh-whoosh. The air is sprinkly.

It's so ugly up there. It's cyclone and hurricane both up there.

I am thinking I'll wash and curl my hair when I get to my corpse home. I'll stay in till midnight admiring myself behind bolted door, the same as would any girl of like pluckish mind. Then I'm off over the rooftop. I'm the Night Prowler from Hades in this burg.

"Don't do that," Mental is going in a low, womanish squeal. Me looking around to eye-catch what he is talking about, for the sound is somebody else up inside his mouth. He isn't though, not going "Don't do that" about anything out there in the wide world's greater realm. He's got both hands deep in his pockets. He's doing it to himself, his eyes glazing some.

I decide to myself I'm not studying Mental. Mental is an embarrassment to the upright species.

He's a leftie, I note.

La, la, I goes, primping my hair.

That bug thing is crawling up my leg again, under the purple spandex tights where it's found home behind a girl's tender kneecap.

It's killing me, I goes.

Jack Dreck is reading.

"There's drought in the sub-continent," he's going. "There's bloodshed in...in I can't say it."

"Why won't you let me?" goes Mental in my face.

This anguish in his.

"What's the big deal?" Mental goes.

The same as he does on other days when Mental's got me pushed up against the cold storage or out by the Dumpster where we are made to stash all the off-colour perishables so's the Food Bank people can't get at that produce to give it to the deadbeats so's the deadbeats can go and have more babies at gigantic cost to us serious tax-payers.

So claims my foster pop, the dictator.

Mental sometimes out there saying while he rubs me, I'll pay yous ten pennies a minute. I'll give yous my white apron. I'll give yous my shoes. But sometimes not saying anything, condensation on his brow, those hips going rub-a-dub-dub, him squinting, his tongue lolling.

Jack Dreck on the loading ramp these times, revving his behind, going, "Don't let her tell you different. She wants it."

Which I did and dint, the way it goes. On my own time, I mean, or with my dream party, I'm for it. Otherwise, though my mind is hinged to the sex shelf and my spirit body is willing, the rest stands pat. Kiss it, the boys going, all this past year since I shot up. But hold off for your true love till yous—you—are fourteen, my pal Dotty back in the Neck goes, is how she views that issue. Her fifteen and already married once, though it annulled and not mentioned in the family chronical except during punch-the-nose drag-outs.

"Give it to me good," goes Mental.

Me polishing my gold anklet.

Well, stand up, I goes to myself.

This ought to keep you, I goes to him. I wipe my finger across the chassis, then under his nose, then move on off the ramp, because our ten minutes have dibbled and dabbled and now it's back to business with EatRite's fruits, veggies, meats. All the glorious extras for the smart shopper.

The wind going *whoosh-whoosh*, ripping and roaring. It suddenly night-time out there in what a minute ago was precious sunshine.

"Oh shit," goes Jack Dread. "There's Crisp."

He is dead right. There by the tomatie load in the back room is my foster pops, Edward S. Crisp, Sr., EatRite HQ central on account of his being manager.

The tomaties bin is all rotted tomatie, juices seeping through the lattice-work. Hydroponic, $1.69 the pound. Foster Pops is sniffing and stalking and smelling the puddle. He is tearing at what remains of his turkey-crop hair.

Him going, "Now what? Now what?"—all grossed out.

"Fuck you all, you are dumbos or what?" he's going.

"Yous are all fired," he's going.

Which is how he goes anytime a minute turns sour, like his little thing is caught in the zipper.

Jack Dreck is whispering this in my ear. Then using his tongue.

Jack Dreck is slowed down since his stroke. He's keeled over one day, I'm told, at the meat counter, his face buried up to the ears in black olives.

I've circled wary of eye around behind Foster Pop's backside since I was crawling and the earth sunk into jelly. I'm easing out the Employees Only door. Eying Foster Pop's flaring buttocks which are like two mattresses stitched side by side.

"Yous!" he's going to me.

"Just a minute, yous bony, long-legged bitch," he's going. The floor is covered with wilted lettuce, close to like being scenic autumn leaves, plus loose taters, onions, carrots, squished melons.

"Hold on yous," Foster Pop goes. He's crossing to the proximity, breathing hard. "Girl, yous signed for this load," comes the bellow. "Why dint yous check it first?"

"Why dint you?" he goes. "Yous been in my temporary employ one week, already yous ruining EatRite.

"Yous have signed your death warrant," he goes.

"Yous zonked out pussy," he goes.

Like although I'm his flesh and blood, so to speak, I'm the last one he'll let get away with even the minutest rupture in the EatRite universe.

I've got my hands up, anticipating the belt.

"Dock her pay," goes Mental, right up in Foster Pop's red face.

Me thinking, Traitor, all the times yous have rubbed me.

When Foster Pop hits me I know I'm going to bounce and I've got my hands, my eyes, spinning around to find where. His fist gets me on the side of the head. I don't even see it coming. Next, he's kicking. I hit the metal door and go oomph. I bounce off binned grapefruit, careen into taters on a trolley. "I told Sen-Sen she ought never of had yous," he goes.

My fabled mother, he means. His one and only sister, dead these thirteen years in a drag race, her carrying me.

He's still stalking the prey, my head ringing. So I just scream out without thinking, Yous smarmy shits!

Yous smarmy shits!

Yous smarmy shits!

Three times. Like what goes for one goes for all, à la the Three Musketeers. Which is not what I mean, though I am not correcting myself. I am getting out of there.

"You get yous butt back here," he's going.

Him laying down his laws, for the close-knit fabric of the universe.

I give him the up yours freestyle digit.

Where to now? my inside head is going.

I'm only in this burg for the school holiday, see? Seeing

old friends, earning the dollar.

I should of stayed in the Neck, my head's inside is going. "What's the matter with yous," goes Pokey at checkout as I'm flying.

I've got angst, I goes.

Out on the street rain is falling like it's meant to be a secret plague. It's so fine a mist it's like moisturiser on the face. Like the rain has come in disguise to mildew the human race. My bootgear is a surface of pin-head bubbles. I'm soaked through to skin. Wind is swirling debris inside smallish pools in the alley corners where the no-home people are in congregation around sizzling fire-barrels. Them oohing and aahing and going Oh shit. Throwing up a merry hand for the groovy toasting and shaking their hips in the monsoon weather, going Marry me, Sex Pot.

Me going, Just say when. Spanking the air. Those old alkies such a hoot.

The streets are like Black Death. It's like meanest night.

I drift over to the homeless congregation, holding tight to my tie-dye scarf from Home Ec. Wind is rocking me to and fro. I ankle up to my best-known no-home mate, Prince. My half-brother, him being of the EatRite chain: a freaky disowned boy now going by the name Prince Charlie Smack. The Smack part being obvious to one and all, from one look at his wasted self; the Prince part coming from how he greets society with hands slung in the dirty suit coat pockets, them thumbs ever hooked outside, a ratty ascot rimming the chicken neck.

"Hi, Butter," he goes.

He's looking at me through red-rimmed eyes, making room as his mates one and all goes, "Hi there, Starkie-Larkie, Hi-yo, Butter, gimmie five!" Smack's grimy hand on high, waiting for mine. "Hey, Broomstick, show us yous tits," goes the rabble. Then laughing like demented.

In no mood, I goes to Prince. Your precious Daddy hit and fired my can.

"He dint!" goes Prince, balling his fists and squinching his eyes.

"May he burn in hell," goes Prince, though I know he

puts no treasure in that idea.

Tomaties, I goes.

"Fucking tomaties," he RSVPs.

An old alkie is lifting me up, hands cupping my rump, this whole time.

Him swinging me up and down. You can smell the pee on him. His whiskers are something; my face will be ruint.

"She don't weigh a feather," the alkie goes. "Eighty-five pounds max," he goes, letting me slide down his frontside to earth.

Yous is one to talk, I goes.

"Don't say yous," goes Prince. "You ain't that stupid."

"I'm stupid and proud of it," goes a handful of the dregs.

A whole week on holiday among the EatRite veggies and I've not added an ounce.

Peaches, six each day, that's all I'm letting in my mouth.

Three, four times a day these alkies are weighing me.

"It was spring we'd picket EatRite," goes Prince.

"Yeah!" goes a handful. "Picket that mother."

Yeah, yeah, yeah, they goes.

Prince's breath is raspy. His eyes is watery. His nose is beet-red and runny. His little goatee is scraggly. All around his lips is scabbed, some festering. Prince is as stringbean bony as me; he's done the plastic surgeon razor cuts to his own self's face to no avail; yous—*you!*—can still see Foster Pop's gross features slammed on him nosewise, earwise.

But Prince's heart is a heart of gold.

Wind is bristling cold. I feel cold through to my bones, though no bug, thank god.

I'm off, it clears, I goes.

We regard a minute the inclement foul weather.

"Back to the Neck?" goes Prince.

Un-huh, I goes.

"You still at Etta's?" he goes.

Un-huh.

The Neck is a burg 40 miles east in Cutt country; Etta is my dead mother's oldest auntie, burnt-out and sliding fast.

"What grade you in now?" Prince goes.

Prince is cosy sometimes. You can talk to him like a

deep sister.

Seventh, I goes. I'm in seventh. Going on eighth, I'm thinking inside my head. Ever I make it.

"Well," goes Prince after a minute. "A sound education is a wise investment."

Ugg, I goes.

I'm feeling right weepy. My cheeks are cold. I'm clapping my hands, doing the foot hops.

"You can't put your money in bonds, then put it in a solid education. Education will leap you right past life's rigours," he goes.

Him a drop-out.

I leave here this time, I goes, I'm never coming back to this burg. I swear it.

Yous is my only true family, I goes. I won't never see yous no more, Prince.

"Un-huh," he goes. "Don't say yous."

He looks at me admiringly. He takes both my hands up to his heart.

"It's been right terrific knowing you, Little Butter. Look after yourself now."

Dead Mama was the one party on earth called me Little Butter. In her womb I was then. Prince is the one party remembers.

"Bud?"

"Yes?"

"Where we going, Bud?"

"I'm taking you to Ginger's place. You liked Ginger, dint you?"

"Who's Ginger?"

"A girlfriend."

"Whose girlfriend?"

"My girlfriend."

"What does she do?"

"She waitresses."

"Where?"

"Back there. The restaurant."

"Do you love her, Bud?"

"Sure, I love her. I love her a lot."

"Oh. Okay. But I don't know no Ginger. Where was I?"

"Your dead mama. Prince."

"Oh, yeah. Right! Okay."

Okay, so Prince unleashes upon my bodyworks a big embrace. I'm totally spaced. It's the first I've known Prince to touch a member of the immediate family. A finger touches Prince, he screams. Touchy, see, touchy isn't his bag.

Then he's fingering his scabs.

Whoosh, whoosh, goes wind.

I've been picked, I goes.

"Picked?"

Un-huh. I'm a School Three-Day Intern in the nation's cap. I've been honoured.

He goes, "Yeah?"

Yeah, I goes.

"You don't say," goes Prince. "What's that mean, 'intern?' Three days, you said? Honoured?"

Yeah, I goes.

"Well, hot dog!" he goes.

Miss Chudd is taking our whole class, I goes. We're going on chartered bus.

"I've always knowed you would make it," he goes. He's beaming.

I'm looking at him, thinking Foster Pops has hit him every day Prince was living home. Foster Pops would chase him through the house in theirs underpants, cracking his belt. No dope-dealing homo under my roof, Foster Pops went.

Prince is sliding secret dollars in my paw. "Take the bus," he's going. "I don't want you thumbing no rides with no evil shits."

He's remembering the family man in the Escort has come at me on the thumb-ride down to this burg. The Escort man has gone, "That's the nicest nothing skirt I ever did see." He's gone, "My guess is thirteen." He's gone, "I've done drugs, yessir, I been around." He's gone, "Why don't you sit in my lap like you was driving, little lady? See if

I've got anything you like." Then that man is driving up a lane deep into piney woods, going, "You do good by me and I'll do good by you. I even let you hold my wallet."

This little Pooh bear on his back seat.

Prince and me stand bunched together breathing the cindery air. We can't hardly hang in place. Wind is whipping like almighty god. Icy rain is slanting down. The air has dropped 50 degrees in zero minutes. Everywhere you look something is flying. It is flying from the roof-tops, going clankety-clank, going ka-boom. That rain kitchen-knife sharp. Each minute or two the screen lifts, letting you see the whole realm clear. You see people screaming, their arms wrapping round light posts and bushes and fire hydrants, the motorized citizenry creeping like cat burglars, and yous—*you!*—can't hear yourself speaking, so's what's the point in uttering a word?

Holding on to my tie-dye scarf so's it won't be snatched into next week, along with my eyeballs.

But I must of squandered a minute in reverie, because when I open my eyes I goes, Where did everybody went?

Prince is gone, and the alkies too. They have been swept away. Even the fire-barrel is gone. A heap of barrels and muck are slung up over each other at the alley dead-end, burning and flaring cinders, the building beside there going up in flames. The fire impregnable against heavens' relentless wind. I'm seeing hurricane, my mind goes.

The wall crumbles and volleys fire anew in the same breath; behind the wall, behind the flames, you can see dense smoke and faces emerging from time to time, then them bodies retreating again. It's ghosts I'm sure. It is a car-park in there. Car engines are revving, some poking along, others hitting the gas hard. Cars are criss-crossing each other in the bedlam, banging first one fender then the next; they are all turned around with none able to see the big blinking EXIT which is clear as pie to my sensors. I move a snitch, running low, and there in front of me is a whole bank of cars lined up and honking. The humble city servant planted in his booth behind the red-tiger crossbar not letting the wise shopper depart until they forks it over.

Over yonder whole buildings have toppled. Street poles have bent. Wires are singing. There's a Greyhound bus on its backside, the wheels spinning.

"Bud?"
"Yes."
"How you doing?"
"Fine. You?"
"Great!"
"Good."
"Yeah. Just fuckin' great."
"Don't use that word."
"Okay."

Okay, my stomach is clutching. My inside's got hands clawing to get out.

"It's our afterlife," someone goes. An unseen woman's voice addressing the realm.

Ugg, I goes.

"There's safety in numbers," she goes.

This tall dressed-up woman steps out of the smoke, on her face a smile like from a billboard.

"I'm cool," she goes. "Are you cool?"

I'm in love.

"In Gunga Din did Kubla Khan," she goes.

We have the hysterics a minute, this party and me, crumpling down to our knee-caps. Us laughing till hiccups set in.

"Don't shoot till yous see the whites of their eyes," she goes.

Us whooping it up, my sides splitting.

She's waving folding cash in the tight fist.

"I tell you, this here raw nature cuts into a working girl's time."

I fix her at can't be past 30.

Fanning smoke from our faces as we hug the walls, holding on to them and each other as we scurry-foot along.

Ka-boom, ker-bam, the realm goes.

"I know where there's refreshment to be had," she goes.

Her chattering away, going Oomph in the blindness when we ram each other.

The sidewalk is rippling. There's swooshing mud. There goes another tree.

We turn down steep steps out of the wind, clear of rain for the second, lamps lighting up the run-off which is gushing down the steps, running up over our treasured footgear. She's packed herself off today in red lipstick, red gigantic purse, a red belt, red stiletto heels. Straps over those biggish feet thin as the gold watch band.

It is dark night in the city and we are the Prowlers from Hades.

Clickidy-clack and splish-splash, we goes.

Roof tops goes ker-bam. Theirs broken tree-tops up and down. Theirs glass knee-deep. People are screaming and running.

I'm whipping after her through a slam-black cistern type thing, and suddenly perceive where I am. I've played with my jacks here when I was knee-high, going, What are yous going to be when yous grow up? Going, Which party is it most whips yous? Going, My mama was killed carrying me, now I'm here orphaned to Foster Pop and Foster Mom, who do yous stay with? Pansy-caking and cooking in mud and playing man and wife, playing Drag Race, when we were not scratching out each other's eyes. Going, This is how yous touch your self. Going, This is how, and if yous do it right sludge will pour over yous finger and down yous legs and yous face will go chigger-bite red and yous wont breathe 'til the cows come home.

"Well, you're a moody one," my woman friend goes.

Producing the giggles again.

Yonder at the cistern's end is a baby carriage flying. Yonder is dead things. Yonder is a streaking cat. Muck is flowing. A hunch-backed man in a light suit has it whipped right off him. There goes umbrellas and benches and flying dogs.

There's snakes hissing along. Even on good days you see snakes on the walkways in this tidal burg. They are so smart they wait for the right traffic light.

Up by a pole is a brown bag. We dread to see what it's got inside.

Go on, she goes, poking me.

You go, I goes, poking her.

Won't neither one of us touch that bag. Then the wind's got that bag flying, unleashing in us both the joyous hilarity.

"Home again," she goes.

Down by the dock this is. Planks and huts and boats bobbing in the dark sea.

The next minute we are pulling out chairs in this wide-floored place built over the whooshing waves.

"Darling One," she's going. "Yoo-hoo!"

It's right pleasant, I find, and well-lit, kerosene lanterns ablaze in the rafters. It's warm. There's a fishy smell, calming to the nose, and below the boards where we sit drawing human breath you can hear the waves slamming.

There's sea-kelp and the odd crawdad washed up in rows along the plank seams.

When waves hit the whole structure wobbles and rattles.

"It's been here a hundred years," she goes. "Ain't going nowhere now."

She's stripping off her wet goods. She's making herself naked.

She's got bosoms to die for.

"Honey," she goes. "The men I've heard say that as they are choking me!"

You can hear whistling wind and waves chopping away the sea-walk. But it's pleasant, I reckon, after our duress.

"I can't serve no underage," goes a man's loud call.

But she and me are taking no notice of lowly men.

She's going, "You never seen a dress-up black woman before?"

I'm admiring her shoes. The label in her dress says Hoodwinked.

My party is looking at her hands palm-down on the wobbly table, going, "Can you believe it? Would you probe this?" Mile-long cherry nails have come unstuck. A lone one clings to her pinky. Then she's stooping her head between them slender legs. She lets go with this amazing screech, me going, *What! What!* She up-ends the both legs across the wobbly table corner, jiggling her toes. Appraising the damage.

"No underages allowed on these premises," the third party is going.

"That's Willard, my love-in," she goes. "Willard thinks gloom is a thing so thick he can ladle it on my plate."

Willard don't sound the least gloomy to me, I'm thinking.

Then she goes to him back there, "Just kidding, honeybunch."

I can see the top of his head moving back there.

A popsicle wrapper has glued itself to my friend's ankle bone. Seaweed and smelly muck and black smudges are on there. "The enemy has struck," she goes.

A slither of glass inches long is embedded neatly in the one calf.

How gross, I goes.

She's picking at it.

Blood is scragglety. Like it's peeping out to see what's going on.

"Mercurochrome will fix that," she goes. "On my side of the tracks it was cold biscuit by day, mercurochrome by night."

The glass has a black one side, a mirror you can see your face in, on the other. She's twisting around to get a good look at herself.

"Look at that hair!" she goes. "Why dint you tell me?"

She's got a headful, rinsed deep red, dear as a Setter dog.

My name is Pure Envy, I goes.

"Yours is all right," she goes. "Yous just need taken in hand."

Me and her clang our heads together so's we are side by side in the mirror. She winks the one eye and together we slam off into gales.

The big toe on her foot has falsy nails shooting out like elephant tusks; the poor other nails are all rough dollops chewed down to the quick. Like in the privacy of her own den she'll sling that foot into her lap to gnaw at them toes till the chickens roost.

Then she sets to work slowly wiggling out the glass. She unscrews the salt shaker top, pours salt over the gash.

We are making gagging faces. The floor is rocking and sloshing. I'd faint, I wasn't pinching myself.

"I be my healthy self in Paradise," she goes.

Blood seeps up through the salt pile, us watching.

"That's enough of me," she suddenly goes, swinging her legs down. "Let's study on you, girl."

My boots have weathered the furore though there's tears and rents, holes and zig-zags, in the stretch hose. I'm ruint. That's eight-dollars at Wal-Mart, misspent unless you possess the quick hand.

The itch is something horrible, I goes, lifting my rump and sliding down the stretch tights.

"No juvenile undressing on these premises," goes the deep voice.

A bug in there has been snitching my skin all day long, I goes. It's killing me.

My peeled skin is shocking white; it's purled, puckerish, tattooed. Wormy to behold. It's past disgustment.

"Honey," she goes, "at least you have lost your babyfat."

This induces a new round of delirious mirth.

I shake the tights and something skitters out.

Water sloshes in my boots so's I begin the big unlacing job.

My friend is under the table, scooting about, bumping her head, going, "Ooo," going, "Ah," going, "Yous stupid bugger, I'm going to git yous." At last going, "I've got yous now, son of a bitch!"

I'm dipping my head up and down, but she's a mystery to behold.

I goes, don't say 'yous.'

"Well who ever heard such a thing?" she goes under there. "'Yous' is a stupid word. Yous won't find that ignorance occupying my mouth."

Now she's back in her chair, opening a palm.

"Dint you say so?" she goes. "Isn't that critter the ugliest thing?"

She's got my bug in the beautiful hand.

She pokes the thing.

That bug is dead, I goes.

She pokes and pries, going, "Show some zip, yous."

That insect is reddish and black. It's got four bent hind legs; it's got two tripod-type jobs mounted to the front. It's got a helmeted head.

"Are yous catching yous Zs?" she goes to the bug.

We have a round of hilarity at that.

Then I'm going, That's the son of bitch has been plaguing me?

Knee to thigh I'm a splotch of red holes and furrows, of wells and welts that bug has made in me. Skin is itching to hop off.

You can't tell the other legs the bug has. It's got my skin in its mouth.

"I think it's a he," she goes.

We cackle a while at that.

The bug is the size of a green pea, but flatter. It's packing my flesh into a hard ball with its front tripods then firing the glob into his mouth.

You can see his eyes are on us. Circling orbs are catching the light.

Suddenly a wing lifts; we screech, clattering back. We are both flinging and screeching the wild screeches. We are slapping at our arms, legs, and full bodyworks. *It's on me!* we both goes. *Git it off me!* we goes.

We are dancing and slapping, feeling it crawling. The bug is zitching first this one place then the other.

We are dancing and hopping and having the best time.

"No dancing!" goes a fog-horn voice.

Willard is settling a tall ice bucket by our table. A bottle sits snug in the ice.

She grabs an ice chunk, sucks it between her teeth. Water drips down.

"There goes love, life, and the pursuit of happiness," she goes.

We uproars ourselves anew.

129

"Pop!" goes Willard with a finger in his mouth. Then the cork.

"Willard was with Do-Wah-Ditty if you remember them," she goes. "Willard, do her your 'Do-Wah-Ditty.'"

But Willard is gone.

"Here's to precious drink," she goes.

She guzzles it down.

Next she's rooting inside her purse, pulling out linty pills. On the table they goes rolling.

"I've got to have these," she goes, "for what I must tell you.

"That there is an usher," she goes, poking one. "This here is more your size, an usherette."

I've seen these, I goes. Prince Charlie Smack moves these.

We down usher and usherette, chased by precious drink.

I see I'm barefoot, boots slung to the wall. We are underwater in that corner, my boots sloshing. My stretch purple tights I see slung over a chair-back above a puddle.

Everywhere you look you see discarded garb. Round and round I'm going.

Willard is sitting on my friend's lap, humming do-wah-ditty in her ear.

"Don't be selfish," she goes to him.

He gropes out a blind hand my way. I'm leaning in to help.

She and me are looking deep into each other's eyes. "I can't feel nothing," he goes.

"Butter is underage and white," he goes. "One is enough to get me killed."

"You been killed before," she goes. "One more time can't hurt us.

"Try your mouth on the haystack," she goes.

The minute she's said mouth mine have sprung up.

I can't believe it's my own self there.

"Soft-talking's good, too," she goes.

Do-wah-ditty, he starts up.

I'm in a swoon, making space for his whole arrival. I'm squinting, wanting to witness the first mouth on me but fearful of jinxing the minute.

I hold his chef's hat. I hold it above his head while he
…then I realize his mouth isn't there. He's off to the back-
room, going, "That's sufficient encouragement for the underage. Let me see what I've got back here I can fry up."

There's a great noise out on the docks. The sea-wall, the
dock-walk, all crumbles. Shipping docks, warehouses, the
whole sea-side is tumbling out to sea.

"Bud?"
"Yes?"
"You're the first grown man I've ever liked. I can talk to
you."
"Good."
"Where are we going?"
"To Ginger's."
"What's her place like?"
"You'll like it."
"He dint really put his mouth on me, you know. That
was wishful thinking."
"Un-huh. I know."

Okay. Then she goes, "Do you know who was in that
other car killed your mama?"

Wind has slammed our door open and flung hinges, door
and what-all out into the heaving realm.

There's bodies out there.

"Bud?"
"Yes?"
"There were bodies out there."

She goes, "Every summer you been coming here I been
watching you grow."

She goes, "Anyway, you lived. Mine dint."

She goes, "We was hitting eighty-eight, going side by
side, when the tire blew. Then ka-boom."

She goes, "There won't no EatRite in this burg in them
days."

She goes, "Them was dark times."

131

She goes, "I lost two brothers to the peril."

She goes, "Honey, you are skin and bones. We got to fatten you up."

She goes, "The bet on that drag-race was $5. Five would buy yous a carton of Camels in them hard times."

Don't say 'yous', I go.

"Yous are right, honey," she goes. "'Yous' is ignorance speaking."

She goes, "The one thing I learnt from my mother was to rinse out my knickers each and every night."

She upends her purse on the table, she goes, "Here's loot, it's all yours."

Out flows the bills.

"The tricks I've pulled for you," she goes.

Then she says a strange thing. She goes, "Dint you ever grow wildflowers? Me and mine, we just toss handfuls into every field."

Mama ought not to been drag-racing, I goes. Her carrying me.

"Honey," she goes. "You are telling me."

On the floor my bug has been busy. It is down there doing something along a twig; now it is crawling up over the twig.

"I can hear its grunts," she goes.

We both can.

It's like the bug must grunt if it's to clear the twig. It keeps on grunting, getting so far then tumbling back. But it's on top and over the twig now and seems to be stretching itself. It's doubling in size, then I see, no, it's something else, because the thing is leaving one part of itself behind. It's crawling out of the one part, the husk or shell part, and moving on away with this new slimy part. Though not fast, with a lot of foot-grappling and grunting, because a long sticky mucous-type string connects the old and new halves.

Her and me are down on our knees over the thing. Our faces mere inches above what's going on, the both of us silent, clenching each other's hand, when the mucous part snaps. Plops of sticky stuff hit our faces but what brings shivers of glee is how when the stringy part snaps the bug is caught by surprise. It shoots head over heels. Ping, there it went, popping up against the wall, then tumbling back on its backside.

La, la, I goes.

Grasping for air, wriggling these teensy thousand legs. Us crawling on our knees to get over it again, then both of us puckering up and blowing at it. The bug arights itself. It starts, it stops, it thinks to hobble off. Then it halts again. It's busy doing something, no guessing what. But pretty soon it's heaved a mound of seaweed up over itself. All to be seen of that bug is the odd leg, the occasional quiver of weed.

Que va là, I goes.

"Bud?"

"Yes?"

"Do you know what that means?"

"What what means?"

"Que va là."

"It means 'Who goes there?'" You were saying it to the bug: who goes there?"

Okay. Just checking. Then she goes, "It's saying good-bye. That bug has done ate of human flesh, now it's saying so long."

She goes, "That there's a hurricane bug."

The pile stops quivering. It's out of sight now.

She fluffs a bit away from the pile with her false nail. She fluffs away more. She keeps fluffing and next there isn't any pile left, only a mere hole going down straight down into wood.

We blow into the hole.

"Wonder is it going in there to raise a family," she goes.

Ugg, I goes inside my brain, though already I'm thinking up names.

"It's heart-breaking," she goes, "what a bug has to put up with."

Then water is seeping up through that hole, and here

133

comes the bug.

It's a drowned rat.

We get up, brushing our wet knees. Floodwater is in past the door and over in the corner is inches deep. It's clammy-cold to the naked feet. Her and me cackle, joining in the delirious embrace.

"Try these," she goes, slipping two nuggets inside my mouth.

We shoot the realm the high V.

I've been honoured, I goes.

"I know it, honey," she goes back, giving me back-pats. "Glory is thy name."

She goes, "You are your mama's very own self. You are her to a T, down to them freckles over your nose."

Down crashes the tears.

"Me and her were two hellcats," she goes.

We laugh 'til we cry, at that.

The water goes slosh-slosh. It is over our ankle bones, rising by the minute.

"Bud?"
"Yes?"
"Here's how it ends."
"Okay."

Beyond the door there's naught but rubble within heaving waves. But there's light to be seen far out at sea.

Is it the sun? I goes.

"No," RSVPs my friend. "They are burning virgins out there."

Ugg, I goes.

In the meantime there's hours to live.

"That's it, Bud."
"Hours to live. Okay."
"You could see them, Bud. Far out at sea. On these little rafts. All the burning virgins."

"Well here we are," says Bud.

Buried Secrets

Patrick Roscoe

Yes, I remember Riley, though that was just what we called
him. We never did learn his real name, or anything else
about him. So I'm afraid I can't tell you much more than
Dorothy and Kay have. But listen. If my sisters seem reluc-
tant to go into the story, you have to understand that
things aren't spoken of for a reason. What do you expect,
anyway? You've been away for so long and now you turn up
with all your questions. And it was so long ago. Still, it's
funny what you don't forget.

You must already know some of the story from your
father; the background, at least. How Michael and Carrie
decided to come out west when it looked like things would
never get better for us in Regina. That's right, 1949. It was
just five children then, your Uncle Donald hadn't been born
yet. Lena and Annie and Lil, your great-aunts, had already
made the move to Brale. And Etta, a cousin, married to a
Keighley, had the dairy back up in the hills. We stayed
with Etta and John at the beginning because my father
couldn't get on at the smelter down here. His sisters didn't
have the space to take us in at the time and of course there
was no money for anything else. It wasn't charity, it was
family. We all did our share around the place, Etta made
sure of that all right. Considering John and her girls, how
they were, not to mention the dairy itself, she was lucky to
have us. And to have Riley. Maybe that was a connection
between Riley and ourselves right there: he wouldn't have
ended up in such a situation either, if there had been a better choice. What am I saying? A choice, period.

It was Etta who found him sleeping in the straw, there above the cows, one bitter morning. This was our first winter on the dairy, and I can't say I've known a worse around here since. Well, that house was just a sieve, the walls were nothing. Imagine how it would have been for this man in the barn, just an old tarp over him, sick as he was. You could tell at once he was real bad. Burning up with fever, sweat streaming off him, shaking. All of that.

Right from the start there was an oddness to the situation in that Etta didn't turn him off the place. It would have been in character for her to do so without thinking twice, irregardless of his health. She was such a woman then. One of the hardest lives, she had; you can't judge. Still, it made me stop to see her carrying a bowl of steaming soup across the yard to the barn, with a thermos of coffee tucked under one arm and a blanket in the other. Etta took it on herself to look after the stranger. She made a rough but capable nurse, I'd wager. Any kind of nurturing from her came as a surprise. I don't believe I heard her say one affectionate word to Uncle John during three entire years; he might have been a hired hand rather than her husband. She'd lock the door if he came home drunk, wouldn't flinch to hear him scratch to be let in out of the cold. And she ignored those two girls of hers altogether, slapped them hard across the face if they so much as came near. I saw it. This was a woman with an arm as strong as a man's, too. Really, there was no way of knowing June and April were hers unless you saw the birth certificate.

So, yes, it was peculiar that Etta went out of her way for this unknown man. He was a mute, you know, for all intents and purposes. At first we thought he couldn't talk because he was so sick. When he got a little better, my father tried to ask him where he'd come from and where he was going. Just who he was. Not a word then, nor any time after. He could hear all right. His head turned when you spoke to him, and I've seen his eyes lift at the caw of a crow, a wind at the top of those trees. But no kind of speech at all. The most we heard—and this only considerably later on, only in rare instances when he really needed your attention—was a sort of moan. To my ears, it seemed like an expression of distress. But don't we say a sheep sounds anxious and a dog sounds angry, when it's just the noise they make and nothing more than that noise? Nothing more than our need to interpret what we can't understand?

We wondered if it were physical. A condition from birth or the result of an accident along the way. Maybe he'd suffered a trauma that affected his memory as well as his speech. Maybe his people were worried sick looking for him. Or he just feigned the dumbness to avoid our questions. We wondered about all of that. You read such things. My mother wanted to have him checked by the doctor in town, but that never happened. I don't know why.

Michael and John did go down to the RCMP detachment to talk with Bob Simonetta. They felt they ought to, and of course they were right. The fellow could have escaped from the penitentiary at the Coast. We're so close to the border, he might easily have slipped over from the States. He might have been on the run from any crime at all. The things that went through my mind. You have to understand how isolated the dairy was, way up in those hills, far at the end of the gravel road, no other folks around for miles. You've never been up there, have you? It was just the most unlikely place to end up, as I've said. Or the most likely, if you wanted to hide from the world.

Bob hadn't heard anything. He called the Coast and put the word over the wire, but nothing. He drove up to the dairy—that same day, I think—to ask some questions. Even with his uniform, he didn't get an answer. The man had no papers on him, no belongings whatsoever. I could take him in for vagrancy, Bob said—and I felt he wished to do that. The situation didn't sit right with him somehow. But Etta quickly said no, he could stay, she needed more help around the place.

Stay he did. Slept out in the barn above the cows, summer and winter, with just that blanket. I guess he used the old outhouse out back. He must have washed and shaved at the pump. Did he cut his own hair? You never saw him do those ordinary things, those human things; it was hard to think of him in such terms. I know Etta gave him old clothes, things of Michael and John that would otherwise have been thrown out. At mealtime she fixed a plate and set it on the step. You wouldn't hear him come for it; he was that quiet a man. The clean plate and the spoon would be there when we opened the door again. So far as I know, he never came inside the house. Wait: he must have, at least the once, because of what happened later. But I'm getting ahead of myself. I might mention now that after his arrival we locked the doors at night. That wasn't something we would have thought to do before.

There was worry for the girls—not for me; I was always older in more than just years. Of course we worried, though that particular fear wasn't in the air so much then. Not like now when it's all over the papers, the things that keep coming out. My sisters weren't to be alone with Riley on any account. Kay and Dorothy were frightened of him; we had no concern there. But you know Jeanette, always bold as brass. Even at seven or eight, as she would have been then. Though he paid her no attention you could notice, she liked to follow Riley around. That tall silent man and that merry little girl: it was curious. Nothing was said aloud, but I think we were all watchful, careful. It was Jeanette who gave him the name, wouldn't you know, that first spring he was there. Up to then, we hadn't called him anything. Well, my sister was always fanciful that way, always naming this or that. The cows. I remember a Daisy and a Daffodil. A Buttercup. Who knows how she came up with Riley, she wouldn't say where she got the name. It wasn't one any of us had heard before.

I have to say, though, I've wondered about June and April in connection with the man. They were always giggling together in a corner with some secret, those girls. Did you hear about the time they nearly burned down the house with one of their pranks? There was some sort of foolishness concerning Riley, I'm quite sure. One afternoon they kept looking toward the barn, then trying not to laugh. The next thing I knew, Etta marched straight into the house and without a word whipped them both. I never did find out why, though I had my suspicions. If I felt sorry for June and April, that doesn't mean I liked them.

Let's see. He was tall and thin, with dark hair. Not the kind of features you'd tend to remember. He must have been in his forties. It's hard to say. He didn't smoke or drink, though I guess John tried to get him to keep company with a bottle out in the barn a few times. Michael wasn't drinking so much in those days; it was like that with my father, off and on. With Riley, it was just the work; he was like Etta that way. And I do know he was a hard worker. Even she couldn't complain on that score. He was up before her with the cows, still moved around out there after supper was done. From what I understand, he knew something of livestock. So maybe that was a clue. And he was handy with machinery. Several times he got the old truck running when it seemed finished for good. I don't think he went to town once during our three years on the place. Imagine. When I think of it, what strikes me most was that there seemed no indication of time working on him. From the beginning to the end, no sign of how he felt about things, no clues of likes or dislikes. Not a smile, not a frown. The weather, the chores, us: from what he let on, it was all the same to him. And I never had the sense that there were things he'd say if he could talk. You have to wonder how much you can know about anyone unless they tell you plain and simple. Unless they have people and belongings around that speak of them. Look at this old house: it says everything about who I am.

You really should ask Mitch about the man. Your father helped out with the cows after school; he had more contact with Riley. I was inside all the time. My mother and I ran that house and, let me tell you, there was plenty to keep us busy. We had no electricity or running water at first, just the stove for heat. Etta got the lights in during our second year and, say, that was something. Now it's hard to imagine, even for me. We had the cooking and washing for how many? Twelve? No, I was home already. I hadn't been to school since the polio, back in Regina. Carrie and I were used to working together as a team and we managed to keep on top of things, but just. I really don't know how.

So I saw little of Riley. When I went to hang a wash on the line, or to the pump for water, I might glimpse him across the yard, out in the back field. Often it seemed I spotted him just emerging from the brush or just disappearing into it. Suddenly there at the edge of my vision or suddenly gone. I'd be standing at the sink over my supper dishes and his shadow would cross the dark yard. It made me uneasy, I have to say. Something moved to the front of my mind, a shape of disturbance that never left me for those three years. The time seemed an eternity, though now it's a snap of your fingers, just that, and a year's gone. But we'd come all that way out west, and things didn't seem any better than in Regina. As long as Michael couldn't get on at the smelter, we were stuck on the dairy. There didn't seem any real end ahead, and I got terribly down sometimes.

I remember once. It was after supper. Everyone had cleared from the kitchen, leaving the dirty plates on the table, pots that needed scrubbing on the stove. Did I tell you Etta wouldn't sit to eat? Standing by the stove in her boots and that big coat that must once have been John's, she'd clean off her plate in nothing. Then she spat into the sink, returned outside. She worked like a man out there. Well, on this particular evening I was resting a moment in my chair before starting the dishes. For some reason I couldn't stop staring at what Etta had trailed in with her boots. Mud and manure and bits of straw across the floor I'd washed that afternoon. Etta wouldn't take her boots off at the door and we really couldn't say anything. It was her house; we never forgot that. I started crying. It sounds silly now, but I was fourteen, everything mattered so much. My mother must have come up behind without my hearing her. I felt her hands on my shoulders, just resting there. A light, warm weight balanced evenly on either side. Then her hands lifted, and she turned to start the dishes. I suddenly felt so light. I felt myself rise and float in the air, all my burdens were left below. My mother had released me from them. She took them away.

I've always remembered that. A moment. You know, Carrie's health deteriorated quickly after Donald; the last baby was too much for her. She could do less and less. By the time we moved down to Brale, into Annie's, she was mostly in bed. I still feel badly about that time. We really left her alone. It became so hard to talk to her at the end; she'd always been quiet, I suppose. I know I felt relieved whenever Lena came around to sit and I could go out with Dorothy and Kay. Being in town was something new for us again, we were still only girls. Oh, but I was so close to my mother. After leaving school, I was with her day in and day out. She taught me everything around the house. It's funny. Carrie always seemed to move quite slowly, yet I'd turn around and she would have got the stove cleaned that quick. Dorothy and Kay tease, you've heard them call me a whirlwind because of how I dash about. I always feel, no matter how fast I move or how much I do, I'm still trying to catch up with Carrie. She's there, somewhere ahead of me, a glimpse through the trees.

What has my mother to do with Riley? What did he have to do with any of us? Not a thing. Except there was a connection. However hard to see, it existed. Yes. I know because of something that happened.

It must have been our last spring at the dairy. By that time, I used to leave the house whenever I could, just a few minutes now and then. The place had become oppressive to me; none of the work would ever amount to anything, I knew. So one fine afternoon I went down to the little creek behind in search of pussy willows. I thought they might look pretty in a jar for the kitchen table. Some appeared beyond a patch of brush, that blur they make against the green. As soon as I moved toward them, my dress caught up in thorns. Maybe it was the wild roses we had around there. I couldn't move or I'd tear my dress, yet I had to get myself free. For a moment I remained still, as if the problem would somehow solve itself.

Through the brush I saw Riley. He was bent over a clear place on the ground. Then I could see he was digging. Burying something. A box, it looked like. I stood quiet. I felt certain he didn't see or hear me. The creek was loud with run-off that time of year. So when I heard Riley moan, I couldn't be sure at all. Why would he make such a sound to himself? I was so dumb, I didn't know what I saw. After he finished, he looked around, flattened the ground with his heel, then walked away.

I waited until positive he was really gone before approaching the spot. I didn't think of my dress or the thorns. I dug where Riley had dug. Yes, it was a box. Just ordinary cardboard, this big. Inside were photographs of us girls. My sisters and myself, not June or April. They were from the time a photographer came around and sweet-talked Carrie into having us sit. Oh, was that a big day. We got all dressed up in our best, with the hair washed and curled and tied with ribbon. Heaven knows where Carrie found the money. But she was real pleased with the result. And that upset when the photographs disappeared. You bet we turned the house upside down, but nothing. We blamed June and April, of course we did. It was something they would have done. But it wasn't them, it was Riley who took the photographs.

I stared at those four faces as if they belonged to strangers, or to people I'd known but forgotten. Who? I couldn't seem to recognize these girls, their serious smiles. I kept looking at one face and then another, as if that would help. The creek rushed so loud, the sound filled my head, I couldn't think. I replaced the photographs in the box, then buried it in Riley's hole. Stamped and smoothed down the dirt, leaving it the way he had. This must have been just a minute, though it seemed longer.

I walked back to the house without my pussy willows. I'd forgotten them. I didn't realize my dress had torn on the thorns until Carrie pointed it out.

During the following days, I couldn't stop thinking of what was buried in that box. I pictured Riley digging up the photographs. Looking at them, touching them. Fingering our faces. Moaning. Despite my ignorance, it made me feel bad in all kinds of ways. Soiled, I suppose. Handled. And suffocated, as if we were buried alive without knowing it. All my unease of those three years on the dairy seemed contained within that box. I couldn't look at Riley at all, not even in the distance from the kitchen window.

Maybe I should have told someone, but I didn't. What I did instead was return to that clearing the next week. I didn't want to, I had to. Like that. I knew the exact spot to dig, but the box wasn't there. I don't know if Riley had seen me after all, if he'd moved the box to another hiding place. I don't know if I planned to take its contents away with me this time. I never would find out. I didn't see those photographs again.

It became a secret I kept without meaning to. I don't know that I ever told anyone, not even Ivan. The longer I was silent, the harder it became to speak. Maybe it was like that with Riley. Years later I did ask Dorothy once if she remembered some photographs going missing. What photographs? she wondered. So. You don't realize you have secrets, then you find them buried at the bottom of your mind, unfaded and unchanged, preserved like treasure placed by the pharaohs in their pyramids. But still alive. What is kept secret doesn't die; it thrives in the dark, assumes more importance as it gains size, becomes immortal as the memory of God.

After we moved down to Annie's, I would sometimes think of those images probably still buried somewhere on the hill. It made me feel, I don't know, as if part of us were trapped up there. As if we hadn't escaped scot-free, after all.

Something had been taken from us, something we never got back. The photographs—and more than that? Had Riley entered the house without our knowing it just the once to take what he needed? Or had he somehow or other slipped inside on a hundred nights? Leaned over our faces, shadowy and still in sleep, printed upon the white paper of a pillowcase. Stolen the sight, burglared the moment. Later, I came to feel the theft had been committed not so much by Riley as by that time and place. An empty hole yawned inside me for the longest while. Then I learned to fill it with my own secret.

I never went back to the dairy, not a once through all the

143

years to follow. None of us did, except Mitch. Your father helped Etta out for a few summers in high school. She paid him, not much, but something for his university. And the dairy's just those few miles away. We could get in the car and be there in twenty minutes. Well. It was a time and place you were meant to forget. That's all it was for, that's all you could do with it. But there's this. The spring after we left, the same spring that Carrie went, Jeanette took to speaking about Riley. When we were all gathered around Annie's big table, out of the blue she would pipe up in that clear, high way she had. Say that Riley used to talk to her. He had told her, in a voice like yours and mine, the names of flowers and birds. For the moment we were silent after Jeanette spoke, I felt the air in the kitchen change. It became more weighted, dense. Maybe this only seemed to happen more than several times. Maybe it was just another of Jeanette's passing fancies; she didn't bring up Riley, in any way, beyond that spring. I've always believed it had something to do with our mother's death, though I can't say why. And now it's too late to ask Jeanette. We'll visit all the graves on Sunday.

What more is there to tell? Etta tried to keep the dairy going for as long as she could. John died, then there was just Riley and herself. The girls had gone. June over to Ymir, where she was living with some older fellow. They had a trailer, I believe, and kids—but not the wedding. April ended up in Edmonton, working in a bar. We lost track. Maybe people talked about Etta and Riley up at the dairy alone. I'm sure they did, how they will. When I got a bit older, I started to invite Etta down for Sunday supper. It didn't seem right that Lena and Annie never had her over. I don't know what the story was there, but Etta was a cousin, wasn't she? She'd drive down in that old truck, still wearing her big coat and the boots. Dorothy and Kay used to joke she slept in them, I recall. Well, she took them off at my door, she ate at the table, there was no spitting in the sink. But she was a strange woman still.

One Sunday she said two men had shown up at the dairy wearing suits and ties. It wasn't the police. She didn't know who they were, they wouldn't say. No-one from around here. They showed her a photograph of Riley, but she wouldn't say a word, not Etta. As they spoke, she saw Riley's face appear around the corner of the barn for just that second. Finally she had to order the men off her land. They'd become quite pushy, she said. There was something nasty in their tone.

That was the last she saw of Riley. For a few days, she thought he might be hiding back in the hills, biding his time until he felt it safe to return. But no-one around here saw him again. Did he take the photographs with him? Did he leave something in their place behind?

No, I can't say I ever wondered where he went, what happened to him. For me he remained that tall, thin man in the distance, silently slipping into or out of my sight. An image pushed into a box at the dusty back of my mind. The photographs shoved farther back.

Not much longer afterwards, Etta sold the dairy. There never had been any real chance of making a go of the place; only her slaving kept it in operation as long as it was. That and the contract with the smelter for milk. There's a story for you. The smelter had been encouraging the men in the lead rooms to drink milk; they had a theory that it worked against the lead, coated the stomach, something. And then they found that the milk itself was leaded from the smelter. All along those poor men had been drinking in more of the same stuff they breathed. Now you read the obituaries in *The Daily Times*, all the cancer coming out, and you wonder.

I think they paid Etta off. In any case, she got enough for the place to buy her little house in Glenmerry. She took a business class at night. No-one knew, but apparently she'd done some secretarial work before meeting John—back there in Winnipeg, I guess. Wouldn't you know but she flew through that course in no time, ended up with 70 words a minute plus the shorthand. Whatever else you say, she was a capable woman, a hard worker. She got on with the new high school, she got that one break. It was a good job for her. She ran that office for years, stayed on well past

145

retirement age. Jeanette used to see her in the halls, dressed in a nice suit and blouse, her hair neat in a bun. The twists and turns that occur in a life. It's something, isn't it?

We never got close to her. She didn't seem able to relax, she stayed shut up so tight. All reined in. I don't think she was ever able to realize, not really, that things were no longer so hard for her. She made no friends down here that I know of, and of course her girls were long gone. I would say that at the end it was Riley who would have been the person to count in her life. Oh, your Aunt Madeleine's just speculating, without a leg to stand on. But I believe he was the one she thought back on, the one she would dream about. Doesn't there have to exist, for all of us, that being to appear at four o'clock in the morning? You always wonder what was between them—no, not that. I'm speaking of what grows between people with time, in silence. What there's no name for, no speaking of. That's all.

Rumours of Ascent

Gayla Reid

They come to my bed with stories. Bernie, for one.

I'm in Odin Hospital, not what it used to be. Bernadette plans irate letters, but I tell her don't dwell on that. Tell me something a bit more interesting, I say.

I should mention right away that the staff here at Odin Hospital aren't real. They don't fool me, not for one minute. I think perhaps I dream them, conjure them up, with their solicitous, ice-bright indifference.

The real Odin, Bernie says, kept a pair of ravens perched on his shoulders. They were thought and memory. By day they travelled the world. At night they returned to Odin and whispered into his ears all they had seen and heard. And that is why Odin was omniscient, a god.

When they think I can't hear them they hold a conference in the hospital corridor: Jen the busy bureaucrat, jet-lagged Bernadette, Merle-Next-Door. The topic: What to Do About Hazel. They've already solved the problem of What to Do About Alice.

I'm being Taken Care Of.

Hazel claims I have ascended into heaven. From Mount Taylor.

Not so fast, Haze. Get a grip.

But Hazel has already written to the *Canberra Times*, describing my ascent. And witnesses are coming forward, to offer eager confirmation. It isn't even the silly season; it's a chilly August and the budget is due.

I call for the newspapers. Eventually a nurse hoves into

sight, dumps them down. Just as well I make these people up. I wouldn't want to put my life in the hands of an exhausted, clapped-out carer, caregiver. That's what they're called these days: carers, caregivers. (Hospital yarn: woman comes into casualty, bleeding profusely. All over the floor, up the walls, you bet. Fibroids, she tells the caregiver. Fibroids, she says again, to the doc this time—weeks have gone by, now at last it's her turn. Five boys? the doc says, scribbling busily. Right, he says, finally looking up. And now what seems to be the problem?)

Back to the *Times*. Martin Wake, level four economist with DEET—Department of Education, Employment and Training, so help us all—had looked out his window at four o'clock on the Sunday afternoon in question. Although his mind was on his long-service leave in Tuscany, he'd noticed the two elderly women in matching cherry-red windcheaters, stepping along the path behind his home that led to Mount Taylor.

Francis Nguyen, pigeon-fancier, employed in a photocopy room at Defence, had been out talking to his birds (probably illegal in that backyard). He too had seen them, the old ladies. So said his girlfriend Debbie, who works at the Belconnen Country Rest. She'd been bringing in Frankie's wash before the damp got to it.

From these anecdotes the readers of the *Times* were able to trace my movements: along the paved cement path among the gums, across the road, over the stile, onto the gravel path, slipping finally through the gate and up the mountain itself. At this point, the path is no wider than a sheep track and is at times a little steep.

The ascent itself was witnessed by a participant in a Butt Out program who'd sneaked off for a few cigs behind the reservoir. (Also witnessing lift-off was his dog, Bowler.) He saw the two old ladies going up the mountain track. Had been impressed by their amount of puff. Just before it happened, Bowler began to growl; his hair stood up in a ridge along his back. Then one of the two senior ladies stepped up into the air. Up she went, he claimed, with a calm, relaxed expression on her face despite the chill wind from the

148

Brindabellas. Maintained her cool (his wording) when one of her sandals dropped off.

Bowler barked.

He kept looking up, he said, as the woman disappeared behind the clouds, then came out again, still going, on into the sky.

Until she was only a wash of blue.

The article included a photo of Hazel, holding up the dropped shoe in a triumphant gesture of belief. It was a shoe, not a sandal, Hazel explained in the caption. Being the middle of winter.

It's a poor sort of memory that only works backwards, the Queen remarked.

So they're out there in the corridor, plotting.

In here, the morphine drip gives a reassuring little burp. Morphine rounds out the edges, it's like being on the bottom of a claw-footed bathtub. They didn't have a contraption like this for Ellen, my mother. Instead they gave me pills to dole out to her. Endone. End one. Named by some sadistic charmer. We wouldn't do this to a dog, Ellen said. Of course we wouldn't, I agreed. My husband Dick, he was the lucky one. Dropped dead filling his water bag. Not much call for water bags anymore, but Dick kept his. Liked the baggy taste, he said. I found him by the tankstand, the tap still running. At first I thought what a grim way to go, unattended and unwitnessed. But now I know it's the best, the Indy of exits. As for me, I'm lying on the bottom of my bathtub and over me are the Odin Hospital blankets. You can call it sleep if you want. It's much thicker and murkier than that, believe you me.

"We have to persuade Hazel," Bernadette is telling Jennifer, "to stop this nonsense. It's so upsetting to Alice."

"What do you think I've been doing?" Jennifer replies. Reminding Bernie who is the negligent party here, the one currently living overseas. After my husband Dick died I came to Canberra. Hazel had already moved here, to be close to her daughter, Jennifer. Of course Hazel wanted to be near Jennifer, the found one.

You won't want all the details, but in the nineteen-fifties Jennifer's father had taken Jennifer away to Western Australia, taken her as far away from Hazel as is possible on this continent. Depriving Hazel of the crucial years of her daughter's adolescence. Hazel spent much of the nineteen-seventies—that bubbling, fractious decade—hunting for Jennifer: beating the bushes, creating a hullabaloo, going on talk shows. Her first taste of the media. (She appears not to have made a complete recovery.) While bright young men prophesied the death of the family, Hazel would natter on about the permanency of the bonds between parent and child. A child separated from a parent lives with an absolute sense of loss, Hazel explained to the cameras, wringing her hands.

And then O frabjous day! Callooh! Callay! Hazel found her, her daughter.

Daughter Jennifer is a senior public servant in Canberra, extremely lofty. Carries a mobile phone in her car. Will be rolling in the bucks when she retires, rolling. Bernie likes to say that Jennifer could run the entire country with both hands tied behind her back. Does in fact run the entire country.

While Hazel was out finding Jennifer, I stayed at home on our property, Ardara. I stared at the hills. I read my way through Bernie's library, all the books she had at university. She'd left them at home when she went overseas.

My husband Dick had his sheep and then Hazel had her find, Jennifer.

Mother was still alive.

"Keep telling Hazel that Alice is in the hospital, and that soon she will be coming home." This is Bernadette talking to Jen. Deep in the heart of denial.

"I've tried," says Jennifer, becoming pointedly patient. "But she sees what she believes." One more time Jennifer's life has been interrupted by her pesky mother. Some things never do change.

"She won't take my word for it," Jennifer repeats. "Even if we could be sure about the last bit."

"She can't go on like this, with her head stuck in the

sand," declares Bernadette.

"Stuck up her arse," says Jennifer, being the more decisive.

Best song title, ever: "It Had to Be You."

Is everybody happy? Bring on the clarinets.

I have less and less to lose. I used to play my cards close to my chest, but I've decided I can tell you. I wandered around and finally found. Turns out the joker in this particular pack is a tiger. Open the door and the tiger leaps. Who said that? Can't remember, not for the life of me.

"She's more than holding her own," says the doctor. Talking about me to Bernadette and Jennifer. Jennifer gets a highly responsible look on her face when the doctor is talking. The doctor is genial but rushed, hirsute but closely shaven, with small bright-as-a-berry eyes. In his spare time, he's a spelio. That's what he says, anyway.

"Goes down into caves on the Nullabor," I say to Bern and Jennifer. "Imagine how soothing and cool it must be. There's shade down there thousands of years old."

I can tell by the look on her face that Jennifer thinks I'm wandering. But Bernadette wants to talk about the doctor wading through subterranean waters. Does he perhaps carry an inflatable dinghy? The doctor looks exactly like a bat. He does. I suspect that as soon as he goes off shift—everyone does these endless shifts, whatever happened to the eight-hour day; didn't people get their skulls bashed in for that?—he hangs himself up for a brief rest. When it's really dark, when everyone has switched off their TV sets and got under their doonas, he's out and about, tearing fruit trees apart. Next morning the possums get the blame.

But so much for the doc. The point is, when he's out gorging himself, that's the time the tigers come calling.

They come down the corridors and stand at the doors, looking in to check. Precise and wary, but not in the least shy. Naturally, the protocol is to pretend you've not seen them, to look the other way.

One of them has his eye on me. Always the same one. He comes to my door and looks in. I pretend I'm asleep.

I'm his, you see.

He's chosen.

"You mustn't mind Hazel," I say to Bernadette. "It's just her way."

Together we watch the evening news. The aftermath of a mass murder in America somewhere. Katherine Hepburn comes on and says that at 88, she is going to join Spence. "I have waited 30 years," she says.

Then it's back to the mass murder. "When can the healing begin?" the journalist asks.

"First the tragedy," Bernie says, "then the healing. Just like that. How about a spot of mourning in between?"

"I'm not dead yet," I say. "So tell me a story, why don't you?"

Bernadette tells me this:

From a distance a young girl glimpses a woman being driven down a private lane in an elegant, highly polished touring car. She has red hair, this woman; she is pale, indolent, languid, unapproachable. She belongs to the colonial class, the class that hides itself from the locals and the fierce damp heat in villas set behind fences covered with dense, flowering vines. The officials don't like her, the ambassador's wife. She drinks too much in embassy drawing-rooms.

In the torpor of this particular afternoon, the woman appears to be dreaming, far away, removed, consumed with an overwhelming ennui, utterly indifferent, utterly passionate. (She isn't English, she couldn't be. French.) She has no friends, it is said, only lovers.

Recently a man killed himself out of love for her.

Another man falls in love with her. (This is in a different city but the woman is the same; it is always she.) He sees her bicycle beside the tennis court, which is itself hidden from view. But she does not come for it. The bicycle stands beside the tennis court, untouched, while he waits. He waits for her so intently that yet another man falls in love with her, compelled by such longing. In the half-light, within the exaggerated, febrile smell of frangipani, she

152

plays the piano. The listeners, those who are desperate with love, must wait for the return of the melody.

And forever she is walking up the wooden staircase of the dark grand ballroom. Wearing a black shoulderless evening gown with pale spaghetti straps that cross in the front and reach around her neck.

Consider the satin, the expanse of bare shoulders.

In the gloom, she goes slinking up those stairs. We can see only indistinctly the burning movement of her hips as she moves into the shadows that close behind her, going right to the end of memory.

"She moves like a tiger," I interrupt. "She has to, it's the only way to travel."

Bernie looks offended. It's her story.

"Into the shadows," I explain. "Into the night full of tigers."

"Right," she says, recovering. It's her version of someone else's story, chosen especially for me.

When she grows up the young girl writes about the woman, writes about her in novels and plays and film scripts, writes repeatedly, brilliantly, obsessively. She has forgotten the woman's name; she has given her another one.

One day, 50 years on, the writer receives a note from the woman, inviting her to afternoon tea in the old folks' home. This is the real woman, you understand, the one she glimpsed in the touring car, going down a private lane, such a long time ago, in another country. In Vietnam.

"So what do you think the writer did?" Bernadette asks me.

"She didn't go, of course," I reply. "Didn't even reply."

Christ, that was easy. You don't get to your seventies without knowing the answer to that one.

All the time Bernadette was telling me this story I was looking at her and remembering how, as a young woman, I loved to look at others when they didn't realize they were being watched. To see who they were when they believed themselves to be alone. I also enjoyed examining their things. I'm not talking about snooping in diaries—I had an appetite for that too, but it's not what I'm talking about—I

153

had a hunger for how they hung their clothes, how they arranged things on their dressing-table. I would stand at the open doorway to other people's rooms. Becoming more bold, I would venture in. Just to touch a towel, a pencil, a dress—a dress was always good, or a shoe, or underwear. Anything close to the body. I wanted to know how life was for them, how it would be to look out through their eyes.

You see, I wanted to know how things touched their hearts. That was what I wanted, when I was young. Nosy.

Dear Mrs. Behan, the organizer wrote: Your daughter-in-law has kindly passed on to me your current address. We are organizing the fiftieth anniversary of the Australian Women's Land Army in Sydney this Easter and we do hope that you will be able to join us.

Dear Alice, Enid wrote: Although I will be unable to attend the reunion, I was wondering if you would like to come up for a break at Tweed Heads sometime during the Canberra winter. Now that I am on my own, I find I am spending more and more time in the garden . . . .

Did Bernadette ever feel that black satin dress, I wonder. Did her hands move over it, greedily? Did she perhaps hold those thin spaghetti straps between her fingers, her throat closing in desire? Of course she did. Feels unique but happens to everyone, every single one of us lucky enough to get a turn at life, to have a go.

The thing about getting older is you lose some of that hunger. I find I have become, to a large extent, incurious.

When I'm feeling well, when I'm at the top of the morphine, all I want to think about is Zoë.

Ah ha! Zoë. At the last turning, perhaps there is always something marvellous and new, and why not? The rabbit in the hat.

Zoë is Bernadette's husband's daughter. A bonus. Life.

I didn't even meet Zoë until she was eleven years old. Her childhood, swallowed up, gone from me.

Actually I'd rather think about Zoë than anything. As I'm sure you know, Zoë is Greek for life. I think that's a wonderful name. You couldn't have done better than Zoë, I tell her father, Patrick. I'm afraid that when we chose the name Bernadette, we were in a rush for religious respectability. We didn't realize how soon it would sound dopey. If we had, we wouldn't have done it to her.

Zoë is going to be a musician, already is a musician. We are a musical family, that's probably the best thing about us, the luckiest thing. Music is what stays with you, snugged around the heart like the finest wool.

Zoë, who isn't even near her thirties yet, has gone off to Donegal to make music in the northern summer. In a country cottage in the west, rented from its German owners at enormous expense—Bernadette complains, but she shouldn't. Zoë's young, I say, she should have all her adventures. Why Zoë has to go all the way to green-and-grey Donegal is beyond me, but who cares? She's got one of those computers that you can play the notes on. It comes out on a synthesizer thing. You can get all the instruments on it. How it works, I don't know; it's a glorious mystery.

Zoë could, as Bernadette is quick to point out, go off to the Northern Territory and make music in the desert, where the air is clear and also full of magic. Instead, she wants Donegal.

My Zoë, she wears tights under messy cut-offs, t-shirts. Orange sandshoes, runners they call them. Glistening brown eyes and hair that can be emerald or fuchsia. Really, says her father. Really, Zoë. Let her be, I say, it will all come out in the wash.

Amazing what the young don't know, isn't it? Can you believe she's heard hardly any Cole Porter songs? Mother and I had to teach her that bees do it, even educated fleas do it.

Zoë's got rings on her fingers and rings in her nose. And I hate to think.

Whenever I imagine Zoë I hear Massenet's *Thaïs*, on the old record player at Ardara. The thin, besotted violin floats out over the tough paddocks and evaporates. With someone as lovely as Zoë, you just have to hope for the best.

Did you know it was because of Thaïs that Alexander the Great burned down the palace of the Persian kings in

155

Persepolis? I read that on the liner notes. I believe he was drunk at the time. As in Persepolis, so in Canberra. More or less. I wonder what Persepolis is called these days? Like Constantinople is Istanbul. I suppose I'll never know now.

Before I came into the hospital, Zoë phoned me collect from the village pub, and she told me she's writing a mass. This surprised me—Zoë is a cheerful little Callithumpian—but I understood where it came from: Zoë is constantly wired for sound. Eating, drinking, walking down the street, Zoë's ears are full of her Walkman, its tremendous offerings.

"Better make that a requiem," I told her. Tongue-in-cheek.

But the young are beautifully sincere. She phoned back, full of plans.

"It will be a Dies Irae to die for," she promised.

That's my girl. Zoë.

Now that the cat's out of the bag, they talk about Hazel openly, in front of me.

"Haze's begun to sort through your clothes," Merle reports. "She's taking them to the Vee de Pee." The St. Vincent de Paul.

"Denial," says Jennifer, "is part of step one in post-traumatic stress syndrome." Sometimes I think that everything Jennifer reads must have tabs and numbered paragraphs. Hazel's going to lead her a merry dance. This business about my going up to heaven is just the beginning. The horror of that moment, the King went on, I will never, *never* forget. You will though, the Queen said, if you don't make a memorandum of it. That's Hazel's Jennifer for you.

"Can we intercept them?" Bernadette asks. "Maybe I could talk Hazel into giving me the clothes to take for her. That way Alice will have them when she gets home."

"No point in going along with the deception," says Jennifer. "Hazel's going to have to come to terms with the facts."

"Fact one," says Bernie. "You don't ascend into heaven from Mount Taylor like you're taking a lift."

"It's assumption, not ascension," I point out. "Christ ascended; Mary was assumed." *Assumpta est, alleluia.*

"It's an assumption all right," says Bernie, getting fed up.

Bernadette describes her visit to our home in Canberra, where I live with Hazel in the bijou bung. Lived.

Hazel answers the door. Takes both of Bernadette's hands, draws her solemnly in. The miraculous event has made Hazel more stately than ever, her still-thick white hair even whiter. Like a country woman on her day in town, Hazel has dressed. A dove-grey polo-neck, knitted navy blue jacket over a long skirt of dark purple. A necklace sits on the polo-neck, blue polished river stones. Nothing expensive but everything works.

Bernie is one of those women who loves good clothes on others but can never remember what she herself is wearing.

Hazel leads Bernadette to the second-best chair, by the oil heater. The room is warm, with big sunny windows looking out on perfectly good sheep country now ruined with little houses. While Hazel makes tea, gets out a packet of biscuits, Bernadette lies back, turns her face to the sun. (Do the harmful rays come in through the window, or does the glass stop them?)

"You should have seen her, my dear," says Hazel, when the tea and biscuits have been served and conversation can begin. "So peaceful."

"Hazel," says Bernadette, sitting up. "I know that Alice's sudden illness has been a great shock for you."

"And so light on her feet."

"But the news is not all bad," says Bernadette, keeping her voice full of tolerant understanding. "In fact the news is quite good really."

"I know dear," says Hazel. Her hands—soft bone and old parchment, like mine—seize Bernadette's again and will not let them go. "God works in mysterious ways his wonders to perform."

"But Hazel, I want you to listen to me now. I want you to listen for a moment. Alice needs you, at the hospital."

"All we need to do is listen," says Hazel. "If I listen, I

157

can hear her voice. And she's happy. A little sad perhaps, but happy." With this, tears begin to make their way down Hazel's grooved face, among the small, benign sun cancers.

"Sad, but happy too," Hazel repeats, busy being brave.

"I know this is difficult," says Bernadette. "But when you see Alice, how well she's getting along, you'll feel so much better yourself."

"I do see her," says Hazel. "I look up to the mountain and I see her. I say to myself, how beautiful upon the mountains."

"You know what I think we should do?" says Bernadette, standing up, pretending to be on the point of leaving. "I know Alice would like to see both of us. Now that I'm here. Look, we'll go together. I'll drive you. She'll be thrilled."

"But she does see us dear," says Haze, who has wiped her eyes. "You mustn't worry about any of that."

Sensing defeat, Bernadette begins to behave badly.

"Once she's settled in heaven, I'll be able to pray to her," Bernadette says, assuming the believer's voice of trust. "We all will." And for a moment, Hazel's face is startled into openness. (*Gotcha!*)

Hazel draws back, dignified. Sinks into her polo neck.

The thing is, I know where Hazel gets this from, this twaddle about my ascent. A few years ago, Patrick and Bernie and Zoë went to a wedding. It was the wedding of the daughter of Bernadette's first husband. Much gnashing of teeth when that marriage broke up, but they're friends now, Bernie and husband number one. They like to sit around and drink fancy beer together and pretend they're both one hundred years old. After the wedding, which was up the north coast somewhere, they had their picture taken. On a headland: cliffs, beach, ocean, sky. Bernie says the north coast is actually paradise on earth. Mother always said it was Ocean Street, Woollahra.

Bernie, Pat and Zoë, all in cream, at the end of a summer's day. In this picture there's a wonderful strong golden light and Zoë is about a foot—twelve inches—off the ground. I'd be the first one to promote Zoë as an angel, but

I can see it's a trick from the darkroom.

I've noticed Hazel sneaking looks at that picture, putting it down in a hurry when I come into the room. If you know someone well enough, you begin to understand where they get their ideas from. It can be embarrassing, but touching, too.

Jennifer has a plan. She will bring in her mobile phone and I will phone home. Mobile phones are forbidden in the wards, they muck up the kidney machines. Take the piss out of them, ha ha.

"Hazel," I say, "just what do you think you're playing at?"

They're listening to me, Bernadette, Jennifer and Merle-Next-Door.

"No," I tell Hazel, "I am not, repeat not, calling from the Vale of Bloody Beulah." Her tedious Methodist tendencies showing up. (Before I met her, Hazel went through a phase of being saved.)

"Haze, this can't go on," I insist wearily.

But Hazel has hung up.

"She tires me out," I complain.

"What's she going to say when you turn up on the front doorstep?" asks Bernadette. O ye of too much faith.

"Behold, the Second Coming," I suggest.

The next day Merle-Next-Door is at the hospital to visit again. (Whatever did she do for fun before this happened?) "Hazel's sticking to her guns," she reports.

"Merle," I say firmly. "Let me tell you a story." I'll fix her: adult content; some violence.

Merle looks up, expectant.

"In the nineteen-fifties Hazel lost her son to polio."

Merle puts on a mandatory sad face. But the nineteen-fifties is a long time ago, isn't it? There must be more to it than this.

"Her only son," puts in Bernadette.

"Bernie here had it too," I add. "But she pulled through. They were in the hospital together. It was the longest year of our lives, I can tell you that.

"Then a few years after," I continue, "she also lost her daughter."

"I had no idea," murmurs Merle-Next-Door in humble, delighted horror. Hazel's daughter Jennifer is expected any minute. I am perhaps rambling?

"Stories within stories," I promise foolishly. But I'm losing interest.

"No idea at all," supplies Merle-Next-Door in further encouragement.

Having come this far, I shut my eyes, exhausted.

Merle leans forward. As if my breathing itself might yield up secrets.

Note to Zoë. The last before I came into the Odin.

Darling Zoë:

Be extremely picky, lest you become one of those women about whom it has become necessary to inquire, "Is there anything she *doesn't* believe?" Never trust a person in private or public life who says, "I want to make this perfectly clear." But if someone tells you they cannot believe the life they're living is their own, they may be capable of truth.

Remember, the *Pietá* was the work of a 25-year old.

You are coming home before Christmas, aren't you? It will be cold and dark there, and here at home we miss you so very much.

He has such fine pads. Forget leather, forget velvet. This boy is something else. I haven't touched his pads yet, but you should hear them, coming along the corridor. They're the softest things. Living quietness. Pad pad pad.

He comes into my room regularly now. Sits under the bed, washing his fur. I wake up and wonder what the noise is. It's him, purring and cleaning himself at the same time. Last night he got up on his hind legs and took a long look at me, inspected the bed. He has yellow eyes, a bit poppy. A thyroid condition, genetic probably.

How do you describe the golden eyes of a big cat? Gold-bright, gleam-garnished, light-filled amber, crushed butterfly wings? The black tunnel at their centre, opening and closing, making the finest, most crafty adjustments.

He was quite small at first. Did I tell you that he's getting bigger? I know he's thinking about me more. Stands up, front paws on the blanket. Looking at me, considering. Sizing me up.

He's an all black tiger. The special kind.

Hides under the bed if nurses come in. They never see him slipping away. For who can disappear as easily as a cat, who can vanish as convincingly? The nurses arrive with their ghastly good cheer, pushing and probing and chirping.

"And the city of God was pure gold, like unto clear glass," I tell them.

"Was it, dear?" they say, slipping in a needle.

"Don't count on it," I say.

The bat arrives after his night at the fruit. "You're looking well this morning," he says.

"Don't look too bad yourself," I say. "For someone who's been up all night." He acts innocent, gives a brief laugh, no extra charge, he won't even note it down on the bill.

They were gathered on the roof last night, the tigers of Odin. Not my boy, he was beside me all the time. Some of the others. Jumping up and down, as a matter of fact. Rejoicing, or fighting; I don't know which. Actually I suspect they had a body up there and were quarrelling over it. Bickering: hallmark of the animal kingdom and that includes us. Limb from torso, like the early Christians in the coliseum. We who are about to die are not particularly chuffed about it. I lay in my bed in pain and terror, he was down below, on the floor alongside. From the way he carried on you'd think nothing unusual was happening. He simply put his head down on his paws and went off to sleep. Pain and terror. Lead blankets, heavy and cold. (In hospitalspeak—*resting comfortably*: drugged insensate; *experiencing a little discomfort*: in pain and terror.) Experiencing a little discomfort, I lay under my blankets, *Odin Hospital* in red stitching on the side, in case you're planning on swiping them.

Concentrate on Zoë, instead.

Zoë, skating down the street of a village in Donegal. Thinking about phoning home, then forgetting. Her fancy new skates are of no use in the soggy lanes, she carries them over her shoulder. She's getting on with her requiem, though. *Dies irae, dies illa.* I don't think she knows what the Latin words mean. No worries, she can buy a dictionary and look them up.

I don't know where I got the courage from. But I did have it. You will find that you have it too.

Bernie has smelt the tiger. Despite her denials, she knows the great game's afoot. She wants to get things said while there's still time. Asks me about this and that and tother. "How did you *feel*?" she insists. A child of her time.

"I simply can't remember how I felt," I reply, to annoy. But then I relent, because what will it matter? I spill the beans, they run all over the floor, I had no idea I could remember so much. "My life is yours," I say. "Help yourself."

Greatly encouraged, Bern wants to know if I have any regrets.

'We're all sisters under the skin," I say. "The sisterhood of man."

"But do you have any regrets?" she insists. "The roads not taken."

I don't have the heart to tell her that pouting about roads not taken is a luxury of the middle-aged.

"Father had a gelding called Regret," I reply.

But Bern is not to be put off. "Give me the names of all the Ardara animals," she commands. "As far back as you can remember."

"I believe Grandfather McGinty had exceptionally clear brown eyes," I say. "You might want to make a note of that."

She's voracious, Bernadette. Greedy and voracious. Feels familiar.

"I suppose you're having the coffin wired for sound?" I say.

Today she talked to me about her husband, Patrick. He's

Canadian, she met him in Italy, his father was Italian. Have I mentioned any of this? Everything is all mixed up, but then everything always was, wasn't it?

Patrick takes her into the Quebec woods, to a clearing on a ridge, to a tarpaper shack he calls a camp.

I'm not particularly interested. I'm incurious. But I listen. I save it up to tell the tiger, grist for the mill: nothing, finally, is wasted.

Patrick points out to her what he sees: red oak, beech forest, red maple that looks black. Inside the shack there is a bed on a makeshift loft, a table, a few open shelves, a wood stove for both heat and cooking. The stove pipe sticks out the side of the shack, curving. In a poster on the wall a man's head turns into a forest.

Close to the shack, Patrick finds a place in the grass where a deer has made its bed. Without any self-consciousness he kneels down, curls himself into it. Lies there, relaxed and replete.

A quarter of mile through the woods is a shallow lake that gathers the light and offers it back to the sky. Between sky and lake, a rim of dark trees. Going down to the lake, Patrick shows her the marks of bear claws on the smooth-barked beech. And on the red maple, nearer the water, vertical lines made by the teeth of a moose. He wants her to touch these trees, to put her hands into the grooves made by the big wild animals. (Put your fingers into my wounds, said the risen Christ, glowing in supernaturally clean robes.) It was a year when the beech had nuts; bears had been rooting about in the leaf litter. Patrick and Bernie sit on the moss-cushioned rocks—the moss, a bright green, holds the light almost the way water does. They splash about in the lake, their bodies slippery in the long still evening.

Back in the shack, they get a good fire going, eat vegetable stew with a French name, drink wine from the Hunter Valley, listen to the news on CBC radio. The sky bleeds orange into red. Patrick stands in the doorway, lifts his head and breathes in through his nose to catch the smells. He holds up a hand, silence. "Blue jays," he points out. "Evening grosbeak," he murmurs, hesitant at stating the obvious.

The dark gathers in the woods and enters the cabin, where the sheets smell damply of pine and, oddly, of salt.

When Patrick comes he cries out in the raven's voice: *quork quork quork quork.*

It is not her home.

It is, without any doubt, his.

When everything has faded from his mind, Patrick says, when they've done their worst with tubes and probes, when they're wheeling him along a corridor on a gurney and he's gone beyond all his adults years—including, of course, all of those with her, Bernadette—this is what will remain: the camp in the clearing, the smell of trees. Tracks in the earth. His elder brother, driving down snowy backroads, taking them there.

The shape of the glacier-scarred hills. Those will be the last to go, he says.

Today, another Patrick story. And I was hoping for a post-card from my Zoë.

Patrick's a biologist, did I tell you that? Complains that kids these days can't spell *alimentary* as in *alimentary canal.* Without spell-checker, Patrick said, they're left high and dry. Like shags on a rock, I put in. Yes, he said, and smiled. Shags on a rock. And you know something? I felt pleased to have someone smile and agree with me. Pathetic, isn't it, how we hanker? God, we never stop.

Bernie had gone back to Canada after Mother died. Back to Patrick and work, getting on the big plane one more time, absence throbbing inside her heart. Back to the university where she and Patrick currently draw their cheques. At the end of the day, she went to his office in the biology wing. Keeping calm, holding herself together in the public world. On some trivial pretext, Patrick took her to the room where they store the skins: long thin wooden cupboards, old-fashioned drawers made of oak.

"We certainly don't do this any more," he reassured her.

164

"These are old skins, most of them 70, 80 years old."

He selected a skin and held it up for her, in the thin December light. He knew how to start with the low-key colours, when to turn it over. At first he held it so that she saw only the head, upper parts, wings and outside tail feathers: the deceptively drab olive brown. Then he slipped it round, brought it up so that the sun caught its extravagant gold opalescence. The body was long gone, but there it was: the skin of the male Golden Bowerbird.

He did this, Zoë's father, he gave his gift with a complete lack of flirtation. It was a tribute from him to the bird, and Bernadette was his witness.

She had walked away from his building, still carrying her own sorrow but thinking of the bird, the golden bird.

I've been listening carefully to all this, to the strange names and images, waiting for what it might yield. And here it is:

This is the gold that is his eyes.

I wonder what Patrick would make of my tiger. As a biologist, in a purely professional sense, I am sure Patrick would admire his strength, his symmetry.

My tiger hops into bed with me every night now. Pawpaws a spot, gets in under the crook of my arm. We lie curled together like lovers. I am permitted to kiss his face, stroke his head between his ears. He purrs to me, he listens. And he does understand that so very much has fallen away. He realizes how distant they are becoming to me and he knows that that doesn't mean I didn't love them, not for one minute.

My mother. Dick, and Hazel. And Bernadette, who will be here after I'm gone, who will want to tell you these things, who will not be able to forget.

None of that feels particularly close now.

Not compared with the plaster spotty dog Father brought home from the show in 1929. It was about four inches high, an impressive size. Spotty dog wore a red polka-dot collar and looked mournful—as well he might that year. I had him on the dresser beside my bed.

Yes, yes, the tiger says, I remember spotty dog. You were six.

Not compared with the way I rode with Father, lifted up and up by Mother, who was saying something about precious cargo. Me enclosed in Father's chest and the warmth of the horse—it was a winter's morning, there was frost—and the smell of the saddle and gums and us racing, racing, and the magpies rising their throats and Father roaring with pleasure. It was one, all of it one precious cargo. It was being alive and moving over the face of this earth.

You can't ask for more than that.

This isn't entirely a pretty story, you understand. I don't want to upset you unduly. But tigers, like all cats, are carnivores. You can feed a cat all the brown rice you like but what a cat craves is animal flesh. Warm and fresh is naturally preferred. So there is bound to be a certain amount of tearing and grabbing and rending asunder. Nobody gives up without a fight, we hang on, we hang on for dear life.

Last joke I will tell, ever, I promise: Be careful what you wish for; I'm finally losing weight.

Bernadette pulls a face at this, so I tell her about the seven dwarves who went to mass in Melbourne; she tells me about the first lawyer to make it into heaven. I round off with one about Pat and Mick down at the labour exchange. Wishing Gerry was with them because there's a job going for tree-fellers.

Bernadette's face is becoming wilder while Jennifer's grows more responsible by the day, gathered and tense with its own considerable importance. Jennifer will have Hazel. Something to go on with. It'll be Bernie who can't cope, who says, last one out turn off the light, so where's the fucking switch? Bernadette who maunders, who stumbles into doors, who asks, Where have you gone?

I wake up and they're standing above me, Bernie and Jennifer, looking at me like I'm a sheep down in the heat and they're determined to haul me up, make me go on until I grow weak again, thanks for precisely less than nothing.

"Go ahead," I say. "Devour me sooner rather than later. Might as well." I shut my eyes. I turn away.

I'm home on Ardara, the delicate bony shape of the tablelands, its slopes clean, lucid and sharp.

A crow cries in the empty hall of summer.

Cicadas have sung up the heat, which stretches across the boulders, lies deep in the dry grass. At night we look up and remember that the stars, too, are burning, made of fire.

It's the end of the New Year's Eve party. We had a barbecue after it got dark and the flies died down. Now there's just me, Hazel, Mother and Dick. The kids have gone: my son's lot, my son himself. Bernadette and Patrick and the supreme Zoë. Zoë wore a pink dress with a bouncy, full short skirt like the ones Ginger sometimes wore when she danced with Fred. A small pink dress. What an absolutely marvellous thing to be able to think of, to remember. And Zoë's skin so silky-gorgeous I could have licked her all over, God yes, I could have eaten her alive.

They have all gone. Mother opens the piano for a few last corny songs. It had to be you. And even be glad, just to be sad, thinking of you. I learned all the best songs from Mother, really I did.

Then Mother goes to the record-player and puts on a Bach cantata: *Herr, gehe nicht ins Gericht*. A change of pace.

I'm not quite sure. I think it's, Lord, don't judge us.

About two in the morning of the new year. By June I will have lost both Dick and Mother. Where they were that night, there is now nothing.

There you have it.

No need to go on about it, as Mother used to say.

But here's Bach, blasting away with such elegant, uplifting confidence and I'm listening to the recitative near the end, to the promise, "God will open wide the gates of heaven," and I'm looking around the room, thinking that I don't really believe a word of what Bach is saying, not in any literal sense, but what a splendid, ambitious, mysterious idea it is: perfect happiness, perfect love, forever.

I tell the tiger.

Open wide, I say.

Arithmetic and the Next King

Yann Martel

The next king was at first well-disposed toward the mission. He came to us with an open mind and a generous spirit and took to Our Lord Jesus Christ without difficulty. I remember that he greatly enjoyed singing. At the time we only had three hymns in Chibokwe. (You must understand that we were pioneers and with Mr. Upton's passing away of fever we lost the Africa veteran among us. I was considered the Chibokwe language expert though I had been at the mission hardly five months.) The King took to these three hymns. He was among the loudest and happiest in singing them and never flagged, not even at the twenty-fifth rendition. The Africans have a very high tolerance for repetition. You see it in their music and in their dance. We thought it a good idea to sing the hymns over and over till not only the words had sunk in, but—we hope—a little of the doctrine. I must add that though God surely saw favour in these good people's singing so pure was their heart and so sincere their effort, they would surely be damned by any English choir master. For there is something not quite right musically about the mix of Christian hymn and African cadence. It's not that the Africans can't sing. They can, admirably. It's rather that they manage to become familiar with the idea of a Western tune without fully assimilating it. In this slight discrepancy—and especially when one becomes aware of it for the fifteenth time in a row—there lies the seeds of great misery for the ears. But they sang with such heart!

It is another matter I wish to address in this report. The King was interested in all we did at the mission and he wandered happily from the carpentry shop to the forge to the brick-kiln to the vegetable garden to the sewing classes, giving them all his royal benediction by flourishing a needle and thread for a few stitches or by participating in the banging in of a nail (the subject who held the nail straight looked most nervous but his sovereign had good aim). It was, however, the school that most caught his fancy. The King enjoyed learning English and he had no compunction at sitting on the floor beside the children for entire classes. I would say he had good ability. He absorbed vocabulary with ease and I might have done something with his syntax—he tended to order about English words the way he did his subjects—if he had stayed with us longer.

Unfortunately, he came upon my class of arithmetic. "1, 2, 3, 4, 5, 6"—he learned the numbers all right, but it was the concept that lead to our difficulties. Once I pointed to a group of boys and said, "One, two, three, four, *five* boys!" wagging my index finger in time with the numbers. He pointed to these same boys and said, "Boy, boy, boy, boy, *boy*!" wagging his finger much too quickly, and then he smiled broadly, as if to say, "Why make it so complicated?" I asked him then if it were not important to him to know that he had eight wives. He replied that it was not their number that was important to him, but their names, which he then listed to me.

It is true that here in the tropics numbers don't seem as important, as vitally practical, as they do in London. Goats, friends, hours, days, children, distance—all exist in their multiplicity without much need of accounting. In fact, the only numbers that are significant to the Africans are Scarce and Abundant. It has a bracing simplicity. More than once, looking upon our mission, surely the prettiest in Angola, I myself have nearly come to agree that anything beyond five is no longer worth counting.

But to be civilized one must master arithmetic. I persevered.

It was a mistake. The King seems to have gone mad over the matter. With numbers—one, two, three boys, four, five, six trees, seven, eight, nine spears—he thought we were casting a spell over his people and his domain. Worse still, with addition—two boys plus three boys equals five boys—he thought we were up to theft. He accused us of being slave-traders working for the Portuguese.

We tried our best to explain that far from being thieves, we were here with gifts, the gift of carpentry and brick-making, the gift of Our Lord Jesus Christ.

He would have none of it. "Six! Six! Six!" he hissed at me, as if the digit were a curse. The witch-doctor, our sworn enemy, whispered furiously in his ear.

The King stopped coming to the mission and from then on we had trouble with that part of the country.

I regret that we were never able to discuss in a Christian way with the King the problem of rum, polygamy and slavery.

MARK ANTHONY JARMAN was born in Edmonton and is a graduate of the Iowa Writers' Workshop. He has been published in *Queen's Quarterly*, *Hawaii Review* and *Passages North*. His first novel, *Salvage King Ya!* appeared in 1997, and a collection of stories, *New Orleans is Sinking*, in 1998. He now teaches English at the University of Victoria.

RAMONA DEARING has contributed poetry to *Fiddlehead* and appeared in *Best Canadian Stories*. She is a CBC reporter in St. John's, Newfoundland, and is currently working on a collection of stories.

KATHRYN WOODWARD lives in Vancouver. Her stories have been published in a number of journals and anthologies, most recently *West by Northwest: British Columbia Short Stories*. She was the 1995 winner of the Journey Prize.

DAVE MARGOSHES has published four collections of stories, including *Long Distance Calls* and *Fables of Creation*, and won the 1996 Stephen Leacock Poetry Award. "Montana," which is taken from an upcoming collection of linked stories, is his fourth appearance in *Best Canadian Stories*.

DAVID HELWIG is the author of more than twenty books of fiction and poetry. His most recent publication, *The Child of Someone*, is a collection of autobiographical essays. Together with Tom Marshall, he founded the *Best Canadian Stories* series in 1971. He currently lives in Prince Edward Island.

LEON ROOKE has written a number of works of fiction, including *Fat Woman* and *Shakespeare's Dog*, winner of the Governor General's Award. His latest collection is *Oh! Twenty-Seven Stories*, and a feature film based on his novel *A Good Baby* is nearing completion.

PATRICK ROSCOE lives in Vancouver. He is the author of five books of fiction, which have been translated into six languages. His last novel, *The Lost Oasis*, appeared in 1995. *The Reincarnation of Linda Lopez* is scheduled for 1999.

GAYLA REID was born in Australia, but now lives in Burnaby, BC. Winner of the Journey Prize in 1993, she has since published a collection of stories, *To Be There With You*, and is currently completing a second collection and a novel.

YANN MARTEL lives in Montreal. He is the author of a collection of short stories, *The Facts Behind the Helsinki Roccamatios*, and a novel, *Self*. He is currently working on a second novel, about a family that emigrates from India to Canada.

DOUGLAS GLOVER is the author of three story collections and three novels, including the critically acclaimed *The Life and Times of Captain N.* His stories have appeared in *Best American Short Stories*, *Best Canadian Stories* and *The New Oxford Book of Canadian Stories*, and criticism has appeared in the *Globe and Mail*, *Montreal Gazette*, *New York Times Book Review*, *Washington Post Book World* and *Los Angeles Times*. He teaches creative writing at Vermont College.